And Everywhere, Children!

And Everywhere, Children!

An International Story Festival

Selected by
the Literature Committee
Association for Childhood
Education International

 Greenwillow Books
A Division of William Morrow & Company, Inc., New York

Design by Mina Greenstein
and Annmarie Cassetta
Story title spots by Donald Crews

Library of Congress Cataloging in Publication Data
Main entry under title: And everywhere, children!
Summary: Thirteen stories and excerpts from longer
books which reflect life in the country of their setting.
1.   Children's stories.   [1.   Short stories]
I.   Association for Childhood Education International.
Literature Committee.   PZ5.A52   [Fic]
78-25932   ISBN 0-688-80215-X

This volume,
in special recognition of
The International Year of the Child,
is dedicated
to all the world's children

Everywhere, everywhere, children tonight,
    Everywhere, everywhere, children tonight.
Children who hold in their hearts, minds and hands,
    Promise of freedom and joy in all lands.
Give them our help as with banner unfurled,
    Children today make tomorrow's One World.
Everywhere, everywhere, children tonight,
    Everywhere, everywhere, children tonight.

—AGNES SNYDER
(adapted from *Everywhere,*
Everywhere, Christmas Tonight,
by Phillips Brooks)

Contents

Introduction xiii

The Leopard · CECIL BØDKER 1

Roam the Wild Country · ELLA THORP ELLIS 21

Hello, Aurora · ANNE-CATH. VESTLY 43

In the Middle of the Night · PHILIPPA PEARCE 57

Shurik: A Story of the Siege of Leningrad ·
  KYRA PETROVSKYA WAYNE 71

Far Out the Long Canal · MEINDERT DEJONG 101

February Dragon · COLIN THIELE 125

Julie of the Wolves · JEAN CRAIGHEAD GEORGE 153

The Black Pearl · SCOTT O'DELL 175

The Bushbabies · WILLIAM STEVENSON 183

Pulga · SINY ROSE VAN ITERSON 205

Sumi and the Goat and the Tokyo Express ·
  YOSHIKO UCHIDA 235

Zamani Goes to Market · MURIEL L. FEELINGS 253

Acknowledgments 265

The Literature Committee
of the Association for
Childhood Education International

ROSE A. BERRY
Chairperson
Department of Elementary and
  Early Childhood Education
University of Arkansas
Little Rock, Arkansas

DEANE DIERKSEN
Reference Librarian
Falls Church Public Library
Falls Church, Virginia

EVANGELINE GUZELIS
Children's Librarian
San Bruno Public Library
San Bruno, California

LAURA HENDERSON
Former Librarian
Lucille M. Nixon Elementary School
Palo Alto, California

BETTY HOGUE
Supervisor
Children's Library of Palo Alto
Palo Alto, California

ELAINE MEW
Elementary Resource Librarian
San Francisco Unified School District
San Francisco, California

EFFIE LEE MORRIS
Former Coordinator of Children's Services
San Francisco Public Library
San Francisco, California

MARGARET POARCH
Lecturer in International Children's Literature
School of Library and Information Science
New York College of Arts and Science
Geneseo, New York

LOIS BELFIELD WATT, *Chairperson*
(Retired Chief, Information and Materials Branch
U.S. Office of Education)
Stanford, California

ACEI *Director of Publications/Editor:*
MONROE D. COHEN

Introduction

And Everywhere, Children! An International Story Festival is an anthology of material chosen by the Literature Committee of the Association for Childhood Education International to give children the flavor of life in countries other than their own. The members of this Committee, working over a period of nearly two years, have read and reread dozens of books and have written pages of annotations and comments. Geography has prevented us from meeting as a whole; but the hard-working members have faithfully inscribed long, detailed, and thoughtful memoranda to me as Chairperson. These I have considered with grateful admiration, and we have had innumerable enthusiastic long-distance telephone consultations.

Included on the Literature Committee are teachers, public librarians, school librarians, college professors, mothers, and at least one grandmother (maybe more by now). That this variety of persons can agree on thirteen books to be represented in such a collection is a tribute to the wealth of literature available for children and to the dedication of the professional critics concerned with it. In choosing such a small number of books, every Committee member had to lose favorite candidates. Selectors could not of course be expected to have equal enthusiasms about every final choice. Moreover, all of us would readily acknowledge that there may be even now in print more colorful and significant stories we would wish to add to this collection. Certainly the final choice was difficult, but the Executive Board of the Association for Childhood Education International provided basic criteria, and comments of Committee members aided in enunciating guidelines for selection.

The Committee searched for realistic yet positive fictional views of life in other lands, and representation of the world's cultures over as wide a range as possible— without sacrifice of literary quality. Our emphasis is on contemporary life, although we offer one touch of historical fiction, just for flavor. And, finally, we hope to reflect the international importance of children's literature.

An ideal publication would be a collection of separate short stories. But literature does not appear to the order of anthologists. Therefore, this collection includes three independent stories and ten excerpts from longer works. The Committee sees this as a strength, for a teacher with this tool will know how to bait children to read the whole from an attractive part.

And so the tales range across the world. A red-hatted goat gives Japanese village children a glimpse of express-train glamour; a courageous boy lifts spirits in a Leningrad hospital. One can also find in these pages a Dutch ice skater and Argentine horse breakers. In Baja California an ambitious boy dives for a fabulous pearl; in Colombia a boy outwits highway bandits. Another story gives a glowing picture of an English family life. In still another we see a little East African boy gain a first taste of market day. Ethiopia provides the setting for a whodunit. In Kenya's forests, an English girl's small furry pet brings luck to her and her native companion; a family of Australian children frolic with *their* pets in the tinder-dry summer weather; a little girl in Norway helps out as her parents switch traditional roles; and finally, in the American scene, an indomitable Eskimo girl learns to communicate with wolves in the icy wastes of Alaska, to save her life.

Showing children of many shades of color, many faiths, many ways of life, some of these stories were first written in languages other than English, some by natives of the countries they describe, some by admiring visitors who are also careful reporters. Children are shown learning how to exchange information effectively with an environment in a raw sense, or learning a way of life. The overarching theme is not adventure only. Interwoven are some universal elements in children's lives: honesty, love, safety, caring about others. In its totality the collection emphasizes the power and richness of diversity as it states the necessity of communication.

Introduction

The children who read such books may in a few years sit around international conference tables with other men and women whose experiences parallel happenings recorded here. Their ability to communicate with each other will depend on their understanding and accommodation, for the purposes of human childhood are the purposes of human progress.

LOIS BELFIELD WATT, *Chairperson*
Literature Committee, Association
for Childhood Education International

And Everywhere, Children!

The Leopard
CECIL BØDKER

*Tibeso lives in a small Ethiopian village.
His father is dead and Tibeso herds
cattle for his mother and other villagers.
When newborn calves disappear, a leopard
is blamed; but Tibeso discovers
evidence that a man with a strangely
scarred foot is involved in the thievery.
Without his mother's knowledge Tibeso
decides to seek help from "The Great
Man" in the next village. There he meets
the blacksmith, who on hearing
Tibeso's story invites him to await The
Great Man, and then leaves him. The
blacksmith's young son arrives and at
first drives Tibeso away. Later Tibeso
realizes the boy is pursuing him.*

The Blacksmith's Real Identity

Wait!" shouted the boy behind him. "Wait for me!"

Tibeso could hear him panting.

"Stop! I have to talk to you," bawled the blacksmith's son as a violent spurt brought him up to Tibeso. He reached out and grabbed Tibeso by the collar. "Why don't you stop when I tell you to?"

"I have nothing to say to you," protested Tibeso, trying to wrench himself free. "I want to go home. I haven't done anything."

"You must return with me."

"No," said Tibeso.

"Yes! My father says so. How should I have known that he told you to stay in the house?"

"But I told you that."

The blacksmith's son let go of Tibeso's collar and moved a twig with his toes.

"He usually doesn't want anyone in there," he mumbled.

Tibeso stood and waited.

"I'm going to get it if you don't come back with me."

"I would rather go home," said Tibeso.

"Father will beat me if I don't bring you back with me." He really sounded as if he would be in trouble if he didn't bring Tibeso back down the mountain with him.

Still Tibeso hesitated. He did not feel like walking all the way down again. "I can come some other day," he said wearily.

"No, it has to be now. My father says that I violated his hospitality by chasing you out when he had invited you to stay. You must come! He is furious."

Reluctantly Tibeso turned and started walking back down. "Has The Great Man returned?" he asked.

"He has been there all the time."

"Your father told me that he was gone and wouldn't come back until tonight."

"Well, his body could be there anyway," the boy pointed out, looking at Tibeso out of the corner of his eye. "It's only his soul that travels."

"Where does it go?" asked Tibeso.

"I don't know. My father says it fetches strength for The Great Man. Is it true that you have seen THE BIG ONE?"

Tibeso nodded. It seemed now as if it had happened a long time ago, although it was only yesterday.

"Did you throw your spear at it?" the boy asked curiously.

Tibeso shook his head.

"Why not?" he wanted to know.

"I was much too far away," said Tibeso, thinking

even if he had been standing right next to it he would not have had time enough.

The blacksmith's boy wanted to hear more about what had happened, but Tibeso was tired and hungry and didn't feel like talking. For the rest of the walk they said very little to each other.

When they arrived at the blacksmith's house, a woman was sitting frying *torosho* over the fire on a big curved frying sheet. She rinsed her hands over some of the ashes with water from a little crock and began kneading the dough with her fingers. Tibeso noticed that it was the same woman he had seen that morning on her way down to the mill with a sack of grain on her back.

She still did not look very friendly. She worked quickly. With short, rough movements she rolled the lumps of dough between her palms, patted them flat, and flipped them onto the hot iron pan.

The blacksmith was friendly, though; much more friendly than grown-ups usually were with children. Even more friendly than earlier in the day when he had invited Tibeso in. He apologized for the rude way Tibeso had been chased out of his house and excused his son's ignorance. This made Tibeso uneasy.

But when the wife handed him a burning hot *torosho* straight from the fire, he thought of nothing but his hunger. He did not sit and pick at this *torosho* but gulped it down as fast as he could. As soon as he finished the first one, he was offered another.

Meanwhile the blacksmith was telling his boy about some straps that he needed for binding something or other to one of the horses. Tibeso only listened with one ear. All packs were bound to horses with leather straps—there was nothing disquieting about that. Besides, he knew the blacksmith did a lot of trading.

The blacksmith sent the boy to fetch the straps, and then examined them himself and selected the best ones. Tibeso continued to cram himself with *toroshos* and wash them down with milk.

When he could eat no more, he asked if The Great Man had returned. The blacksmith glanced at the closed door on the other side of the road and said, "Not yet."

Tibeso resigned himself to waiting; it was still not dark. A little later he got up because he wanted to go out to the road and look around.

"You'd better stay in here," the blacksmith called after him.

"I just want to see if he's coming," answered Tibeso through the doorway. "The sun is almost down now."

"It's better that you wait for him in here," the blacksmith answered, and there was something in his tone that made Tibeso do as he said, although it seemed unreasonable. If he was going to speak to The Great

Man, it made better sense to be waiting there on the spot when he appeared.

"He isn't coming today," continued the blacksmith.

How could the blacksmith be sure about that? Tibeso looked askance at him.

"I told you that you can sleep here tonight," the blacksmith added. To Tibeso it sounded more like an order than an offer.

"Yes. Thank you," he said obediently, wishing that he had not turned around and come back.

At that very instant The Great Man stepped out of his door into the yard.

"Oh, but there he is!" Tibeso exclaimed happily, and started to get up.

"You just stay here." The blacksmith's big fist quickly shoved him back.

"But he's there!" Tibeso protested.

The Great Man stretched and gazed up at the sky, as if he were waking up from a long sleep. Tibeso tried to get up, intent on carrying out his errand, but this time the blacksmith's fist knocked him down flat on the floor. At once the smith ordered the sullen woman to fetch the door, cover the opening, and bar it tight.

"But I have to speak to him—about the leopard!" Tibeso shouted.

The blacksmith put his hand over Tibeso's mouth.

"The leopard—I am the leopard," he said, leering at Tibeso.

Tibeso did not understand what he meant. He fought frantically to get loose, but he could not cope with the hefty blacksmith, and although he kicked as hard as he could, twisted and wrenched, he could not prevent the woman from putting his hands into a noose behind his back and tightening it. She then tried to get hold of his feet, but the blacksmith had to help her.

With one hand still pressed over Tibeso's mouth, the blacksmith kneeled, turned his back toward Tibeso's head, and reached out and grabbed Tibeso's feet with his other hand. His sandals slipped off and the soles of the blacksmith's feet stared Tibeso in the face.

Tibeso stiffened.

The scar!

The firelight shone directly on it, and Tibeso, paralyzed, stopped fighting. Thoughts whirled around in his head.

That was the scar. He would recognize it anywhere. The blacksmith was the cattle thief! It was the blacksmith who roamed about and stole people's animals during the night—and let the leopard take the blame.

And now he, Tibeso, the only one who knew, was captured.

His feet and hands were tightly bound by the leather

straps. Wild and desperate, he bit the blacksmith's palm.

With a roar the man drew his hand back, and for a second Tibeso's eyes met the terrified stare of the blacksmith's son. Then the blacksmith threw his big *gaby* (a very thin, handwoven white cotton toga that both men and women wrap around their shoulders) over Tibeso and wrapped it around his head so many times that he could hardly breathe. Tibeso tried to scream, but the sound was muffled in the layers of cloth. He realized that he had walked straight into a trap.

For a long time he lay tied up on the floor, regretting that he had ever left home. He should have told someone, at least his mother so that she would know where he was and could search for him. The thought of his mother made him cry, and his tears drenched the blacksmith's *gaby*.

He could not imagine what the blacksmith was going to do to him, but he was sure that it would be something bad. A cattle thief who was caught did not have a pleasant time of it. Maybe the blacksmith had done other things that were even worse, and if they became known, he might be hanged from the gallows. Obviously the blacksmith would want to get rid of anyone who knew too much. Tibeso turned cold with fear when two pairs of hands lifted him up and carried him outside.

The air was already cool, and the boy guessed that it had now grown too dark for anyone to see what the blacksmith and his wife were doing. He was flung cross-wise over the back of a horse and bound fast as if he were a sack of grain to be brought to the market and sold. So this was why the blacksmith needed the straps.

No one spoke. The hands worked together in silence as they lashed his body to the horse, slipping the straps under its belly, then yanking them tight. They were taking no chances; they didn't want him to fall off.

Did they intend to sell him? Were they going to take him to a market and sell him to a stranger from another part of the country where the blacksmith wasn't known? Tibeso had never heard of anyone being sold in that way—not boys at least.

Under the *gaby* Tibeso thought of different possibilities and finally decided that it would be most practical for the blacksmith to kill him. The thought was not a pleasant one.

When the horse started moving, Tibeso could hear another horse beside it. That would be the blacksmith. Probably they were going to travel a long distance. Otherwise the blacksmith would have walked. Tibeso tried to figure out which way they were riding. They had started in the direction of the big town, out on the plain where the big market was, but before they had gone very far, they turned off the road and onto very uneven ground.

The other horse was in front now, so they were most likely riding on a path. The blacksmith seemed to be in

9

a hurry and kept up a good pace. Tibeso soon got a pain in his stomach from hanging over the bony back of the horse. Now and then he tried to move a little, but he was lashed so tightly that there was no way he could change his position. He had to give up and stay as he was.

The blacksmith rode and rode. The path seemed to twist and turn, and after a while it was impossible to keep track of which direction they were headed. Tibeso had no idea how long he hung like that, but he was sure that the night was already far advanced when he was finally unloaded and dumped onto the ground. Since his arms and feet were still tied together, he could do nothing to break his fall.

The blacksmith led the horses away. Tibeso thought he was going to be left there on the ground and that the blacksmith would ride home again. But suddenly the blacksmith returned and stumbled over Tibeso's body as if he did not remember where he had left the boy, or as if it were so dark that he couldn't see anything. Growling, he heaved Tibeso up by the shoulders and half-dragged, half-carried him across the rough ground. Tibeso's heels bumped helplessly behind him and a dense forest of nettles brushed over his naked arms and legs. He could not help himself.

Worse was his fear of where they were going. Tibeso listened in vain through the many layers of *gaby* for the sound of running water, for it seemed likely that he would be thrown into a river. But he did not hear any water.

Instead something hard scraped against his side and his heels bounced over piles of sharp rubble. The blacksmith let go. Stiff and afraid, Tibeso lay on the rough, uncomfortable surface, waiting for what would happen next. A foot kicked his aching body contemptuously, as if it were already a carcass, and the *gaby* was ripped off his head with a couple of heavy-handed jerks. Tibeso could breathe freely again, but when he did, he was aware of the strange, sour smell of old soot—a harsh smell of mold and decay that he knew and yet didn't know.

About him it was dark. He couldn't see anything, but it smelled almost as if he were in some kind of house. The blacksmith kicked him again, as if he was trying to make sure that someone was still lying there. Tibeso moaned.

"Serves you right," said the blacksmith. "That's what happens when you stick your nose into other people's business. I don't think you're going to do that again."

Tibeso did not answer.

"Now you can stay here," said the man.

Tibeso still did not reply. He was much too confused and frightened.

The blacksmith pricked him slightly with the point of a spear. "If I were to do you justice I would stick this straight through you," he said, "but I think I'll just leave you here. Then no one can say that I was the one who killed you."

Tibeso shuddered. With a snort the blacksmith broke the shaft of the spear and threw the pieces down beside him.

"The hyenas will take care of the rest," he said, and left.

Tibeso heard the footfalls disappear, and then the beating of horses' hooves off into the night. Only the sour smell remained and the whistling of the wind in the tall, thick nettles.

He was completely alone.

Never before had he been so alone as now.

Far, far away a pack of jackals howled at the heavens.

The Dead Village

Tibeso lay there for a long time listening out into the darkness, hearing nothing, and waiting for the blacksmith to come back. But he did not return. Slowly it dawned on Tibeso that he had been abandoned, that he was going to remain lying there.

And die of starvation.

And be eaten by wild beasts.

And never go home again.

Then he realized how desolate he was and what the terrible consequences were. No one would come for him

—only the blacksmith knew where he was and the black-smith would not be back.

Beside himself with fear, Tibeso tried to work his hands loose, but even though the blacksmith's straps might not have been very good ones, they were too strong for his tired arms. It did not matter how much he struggled and tore at them, the straps held. He could not work his feet free either.

It was impossible. Tibeso began to cry. Deep, convulsive sobs broke loose in him almost without his being aware of it, and the sound alarmed him. It was much too loud in the stillness of the night. They might hear him—the animals. And what if they had already discovered where he was? Fright choked his sobs, and again he lay quiet, straining his ears against the stillness, hearing nothing but distant baying and the wind in the nearby nettles.

When he turned his head, he could see a light area in the sky, a square that was not as black as the rest. So he really was in a house. The square must be a doorway. Tibeso felt both relieved and frightened by his discovery, for it was better to be in a house when it was dark outside; but what kind of house was it—a house where nobody lived? He stared at the opening until his neck hurt. Then he tried to turn over so he could lie in a more comfortable position, but there was rubble everywhere, and the more he twisted and turned and stirred up the debris under him, the more penetrating the smell of old soot became. It was useless. He would have to stay as he was until dawn.

Then maybe he could shout.

The thought was comforting. Where there was a house, there had to be a road, and where there was a road, people would be passing by sooner or later. Somebody would hear him and come and help.

He lay quietly waiting for day to begin. His hands tingled because he could not move them, and his head and stomach ached from hanging over the horse's back for so long; now and then he shivered as if he had a fever.

The open patch in the wall slowly grew paler. When it was finally light enough for people to be moving about outside, he began to shout. He shouted as loud as he could, shouted and shouted—listened and shouted again.

No one answered. No one came to find him.

Tibeso continued to shout until he got dust and dirt into his throat and had to cough. All the while he kept looking around him. It was a dead house. He could see that nobody had lived there for a long time. The clay had loosened and fallen off the walls, and in the middle of the room a whole partition had collapsed. It was on the remains of this wall that he was lying, and underneath the pieces was an old hearth. He could smell it.

The woven door lay inside the opening, completely ruined, for one whole end of it had rotted away. From the ceiling big heavy cobwebs swung slowly with the drafts. It had been a fine, spacious house once, much better than the one Tibeso lived in; but now there were holes in the roof and the thatch had started to cave in. Tibeso knew very well what was said about such a house.

When he craned his neck he could see openings into several other rooms, dark places where daylight did not penetrate and from which an evil odor seeped out. Something dangerous dwelt in there, something that had forced the people to move elsewhere. Tibeso breathed very carefully and tried not to see what was in the other rooms.

Among the fragments of the crumbled wall were shards of black pots, and sticking out from under the clumps of fallen clay were bits and corners of old hides. He could clearly see the marks of animal teeth on some of them.

Hyenas, he thought. They came into the house at night when they were hungry. He shouted again, hoping that somebody might hear.

When he lifted his head from the ground, he could see several other things—a black horn spoon trodden into the floor, broken calabashes, more hides, and a long quill from a porcupine.

Why hadn't the people taken their belongings with them when they left? Or was this one of those houses where people got a disease in the chest and grew thinner and thinner until they died?

Old people said that ghosts lived in such houses and that one should not enter them, because it was bad for the stomach. But the blacksmith had entered this one.

Tibeso yelled. His voice was hoarse from fear, from shouting, and from the dust he stirred up from the floor. Was there really nobody at all to hear him?

What if they thought he was a ghost? Then they wouldn't come.

He ought not to breathe in a house like this, he knew that. He might get a disease in the chest. Tibeso coughed. Then he kept very still for a long time. He lay listening and hoping for the sound of footfalls or clattering hooves.

Outside the door, the tall, dense nettles swayed in the wind, barring the view. It was not a place to which people often came. Farther off there were trees. No cock crowed, no cow lowed. All he could hear in the heavy, oppressive silence was the sound of his heart beating against his chest, as if it were a drum. Tibeso was afraid of the silence.

Slowly the sun crept up over the roof. Nothing happened, and hunger and thirst began to torment Tibeso. He wept silently, licked his tears, and whimpered like a puppy. But no one came. Gradually he understood the terrible truth, that he would have to lie there yet another night.

He would not have believed it, not deep down inside him. What if beasts entered the house when it got dark? Or something came out from the other rooms?

Never before had he been so afraid, not even when he had seen the leopard. He felt for the amulet with his chin, hoping that it would protect him from the evil things he was breathing in. Although he breathed very carefully, he could still taste the sour smell.

Tibeso looked at the spear. It was his own, but having it was no help—even if his hands had been free, he could not have used it. It was the one the blacksmith had broken before he left, and now it was quite useless. Outside, darkness slowly settled in.

For a long time he lay waiting for something to pounce on him. It was as if the night did not enter by the door, but came instead from the black openings to the back rooms. At home in his own village all the houses were round and had only one room and one door. He was not used to several openings, and he had the feeling these doors were watching him. But nothing happened.

Then suddenly he woke up and knew that he had been sleeping. Something was moving out in the nettles.

It was approaching.

Tibeso was sure that something was coming toward the door, something sniffing along the ground following the blacksmith's tracks. He tensed and held his breath. It hesitated in the doorway, crept in, and sniffed stealthily along the walls, coming closer and closer.

Lying half on his side and half on his back, Tibeso pulled his legs up, trying to make himself as small as possible. Soundlessly he moved his knees up until they touched his breast where the amulet lay, and he sensed how small he really was. Even so, a snout came near and sniffed inquisitively at his feet.

Tibeso screamed and straightened his legs with a quick thrust. His feet hit a hard, hairy thing so forcefully that it rolled away over the rubble. It was an animal.

Tibeso felt a certain sense of relief. There had been a snout and a thin, hairy body, and whatever it was it had made a sound when he kicked it. A ghost was not like that. He did not know exactly what ghosts were like, only that they must be different from anything else he knew. He pulled his knees up ready to kick again, but the animal had disappeared through the doorway.

Could it have been a hyena? And if so, why hadn't it bitten him? Tibeso thought hyenas were bigger, but it could have been a small one.

An immense feeling of satisfaction spread through him. He had kicked the beast, and it had gone away. And he would kick it again if it came back.

His determination grew, the will to fight for his life. With his tied hands he groped behind him on the floor.

He pulled himself along, a little at a time, and continued searching. Even a broken spear was better than nothing. He got hold of the piece of the shaft he was looking for, the one to which the blade was attached, and he closed his hand around it gratefully. Recently he had whetted the edge on the flat stones in the brook, and if the blacksmith had not struck it against a stone, it ought to be sharp as a knife still.

A thought flared up in him like a fire in the middle of the darkness.

What if he could cut himself free? What if he could, one way or another, manage to cut through the leather straps?

Carefully he lay down on his back with the spear shaft under him. The edge of the blade lay against the strap that bound his ankles, and he tried to saw himself free. It was not easy. The strain of moving his feet back and forth made his stomach ache, and he was forced to rest often; but the feeling that he had a chance gave him strength. It did not matter that he cut the skin on his ankles as much as he cut the straps with which he was tied.

He worked doggedly, almost forgetting the beast that had been there, forgetting his hunger and his thirst. He had to succeed. He was not going to lie there and die. Everything in him concentrated on cutting his feet free. There was just one strap that had to be cut. He winced each time the spear slipped. He sawed and sawed, and was about to give up from sheer exhaustion when the strap finally snapped.

He wriggled free.

Roam the
Wild Country

ELLA THORP ELLIS

Horse Breaking

It was late afternoon before Uncle Epifanio finally told Martin he might go on down to the corral.

"Go," he said casually so that the other ranch hands might not sense his pride and discover the secret. Martin nodded and left the pasture without a word. How could he tell his uncle that it was too late? Every year of his life Martin had dreamed of the glorious day when he would help break his first horse, when he would ride segundo before all the ranch and do a man's work.

He was only thirteen and would be the youngest segundo in the history of the ranch. Still, it was too late. It was not that he was afraid. Martin knew he would do well. He had been trained from birth for just this day. But would he be riding segundo today if it were not for the drought? That was the question, and the problem.

If only Epifanio had called him last year when the pampa was green and lush, before all northern Argentina had become a dust bowl. He looked out over the prairie stretching as far as he could see in every direction. Usually when he did this, he felt as if he were in an ocean with the afternoon wind moving the pampa grass like a tide, a rich tide that nourished the finest horses and sheep in all Argentina, with plenty to spare. But today there was only a mean stubble a few inches high, too little for a hot wind to move or a hungry horse to forage. The premature seeds crackled like firecrackers across the thirsty land. There would be no seed left for next year. Perhaps there would be no herd to graze either, for this was the worst drought in fifty years, and no man dared look ahead.

As Martin walked, dust rose up in clouds so that his path swirled like a small cyclone. He looked through the dust toward the sun, a relentless monster, and toward the shiny black birds tirelessly circling the flat blue sky. "Only the vultures rejoice," he said bitterly. He had heard that vultures had already attacked the herd of their neighbor. They had not even the honor to wait until death.

But what of his honor? Horses were being broken that the Roca Ranch would normally keep another year, so they could be sold early rather than have their tongues thicken with thirst. He owed his early chance to ride segundo to the fact that they must break more horses this year. That was no way to begin. If only he could find some way to save the whole herd, *then* he would be a great gaucho like Epifanio and today would be the beginning of an honorable career.

Epifanio, second in command only to Don Jaime, who owned the ranch, was the domador, the man on the Roca Estancia who broke horses; only one man in ten thousand had the instinct to do this properly. Don Jaime said it was an art.

If the breaking was cruel, it could ruin the spirit of a fine animal and he would be of no more use than a plow horse. On the other hand, if a horse was not taught that man was his master forever, then this horse was a danger to itself, its rider, and the whole herd. This was particularly true of the high-spirited and sensitive Arabian, who was always a leader and therefore must be dependable. The Roca horses would be ridden on ranches and race tracks and on state occasions all over the world. Epifanio had told Martin that a good domador must think like a man and react like an Arabian; and it was also true that a bit of the domador must remain with each horse he broke.

To Martin it seemed that Epifanio thought like a saint and reacted like a stubborn mule. Once he decided something, no one in all Argentina could change his mind.

"In this I am different, for I listen to others," Martin shouted aloud to the dust. Everyone on the ranch said he and his uncle were alike as two peas. Both had the sharp features and haughty silence of the hawk. Both had unexpectedly soft brown eyes. Both were thin and quick as a hungry puma. Martin had heard these things said over and over, but lately there had been one more comment. "The young hawk is a foot taller than the old one!" Martin was generally proud to be like his uncle. He was so proud that he struggled to be silent and strong, though he often wanted to chatter like a parrot. But he was even prouder to be a foot taller than Epifanio!

"And still growing." Martin walked briskly now, he felt better. It was so hot it seemed you were in purgatory. Dust ran in your very blood. But the horse breaking went on. The doma this afternoon would be as it had been for more than a hundred years on the Roca Ranch. Droughts came and went but the life of the ranch and its heart, which was the breaking and training of champion horses, went on. Suddenly Martin felt it always would. He did not know how they would save the horses, but he felt there would be a way. Then his victory today, if he did well, would have meaning. One day he might still be a domador like his uncle. This was the first step, as it had always been.

Now Martin was excited again, as excited as he had always felt he would be when he rode segundo. What a crowd there was down at the corral! Everyone on the whole ranch must be eating the dust of the corral this afternoon. Did they know a new segundo was riding? No, that was not possible. Only Don Jaime and Epifanio knew. The others were just there to think about something other than the drought.

It would be his task to ride close to his uncle, so that in case of an accident he could rescue his uncle and control the wild horse. He and Epifanio had practiced a thousand times, but still there was a chance of disaster. He could suddenly forget everything, and not be able to move. Somebody might scream and frighten the horse. . . . One mistake and the entire ranch would say he was a conceited boy trying to do a man's work. He could hear them now. His thin, dark face was defiant and wistful as he scanned the crowd.

He saw his friend Carlos with his brother, Alonso, who was just back from the University in Buenos Aires and thought he knew everything. They were Don Jaime's sons. *Qué cosa.* It looked as if Don Jaime's entire family would watch the doma: not only the married daughters and sons and their screaming children but the three elderly aunts who had watched a thousand domas and would be very critical.

Martin frowned. This was something he did not like, this careful tradition. He knew it would help his uncle if he could go into the corral and talk gently to the horse first, as the Indians did with their animals. But he could not do this because this was not the way horses were broken in Spain three hundred years ago. The Indians had discovered a great many new ways to tame horses, Martin believed, that were better than some of the old ways. But he could not convince his uncle or anyone else on Estancia Roca of this. Don Jaime's aunts would

see and judge the same ceremony they had seen for
seventy years, could have seen for three hundred years.
They would not welcome change. Like most people in
Argentina they believed in fate, and changing the ceremony was tempting the fates.

He strained to see which horse it would be. He saw
his own mount, Gatito, tied by a post. Epifanio was
astride his black stallion. Epifanio rode only black stal-
lions and owned half a dozen. But the wild horse had
not been brought down yet. No matter; it would be a
friend. Martin and Carlos took them all out to pasture
every morning and brought them home every evening.

Here it was! The crowd applauded as two gauchos
led a young golden mare into the corral—one of Martin's favorites. She carried her tail high and arched her
long neck, as she docilely allowed herself to be led into
the corral and admired. She was a small horse, but deep
in the chest, with a short back and level long hindquar-
ters. The afternoon sun shone brilliantly on her golden
chestnut coat. She looked around out of enormous black
eyes, frightened by all the people but trusting still.
"*Pobre*," Martin thought, "*pobre!*" What a stupid cus-
tom it was that kept him from comforting that poor
mare now. How much easier it would have been for
everyone. But no, that would be changing something,
and nothing ever changed in Argentina. Not even the

weather. Night and day and month after month it burned the land and parched the animals and caked everything with dry mud.

Epifanio nodded to him. Martin started toward the corral. Though Martin only helped his uncle after the horse was used to the bit, it was also traditional for the domador and segundo to enter the corral together. He hoped the horse sensed a friend near. The audience gasped. Martin noticed the old aunts whispering excitedly to each other.

"*Hola*, Martin! What are you doing?" called Alonso.

"Playing tennis," he called back as his uncle dismounted and raised his arm solemnly.

"We will try a new segundo for the Estancia Roca," Epifanio announced.

"The fledgling hawk is ready to try his wings," Don Jaime said.

"But, he already soars higher without leaving the ground," a gaucho shouted, referring to his height. The crowd laughed.

"Ah, but the soul is truer than the eye, and perhaps even today we shall see how tall he really is," Epifanio retorted.

"A moment of truth! A moment of truth!" the crowd yelled.

"On his first day, for shame. Have you no patience?" one of the aunts cried.

Martin thanked her with a smile. He did not want a moment of truth today either, not yet. There was time for that when he was ready and experienced. The point where a horse was actually broken and finally obeyed the domador was considered the moment of truth. It was like the moment of truth in a bullfight because it was a time when a man finally understood the extent both of his courage and his skill. This occurred for the domador every time he broke a horse, and was why a good domador was respected above all men on an Argentine ranch. But a moment of truth occurred for a segundo only if there was some accident that forced him to take over. The crowd always loved this because everyone knew a domador would do well, but no one knew if the segundo had the courage to break a horse—especially this segundo, Martin thought.

"We do not need a moment of truth to know he is very tall indeed if he has been trained by his uncle Epifanio," another aunt added graciously.

"Hola, hola!" Everyone applauded this compliment.

Don Jaime held up both arms for silence. *"Basta,* enough," he said. "We begin."

Epifanio also raised his hand and the crowd became absolutely silent. He lifted the latch to the corral, and he and Martin stepped inside. From this moment no one must say a word. If a baby cried, it must leave. If a man coughed, he must leave. "If a man died, he must do it without a death rattle," was the old saying for the silence required during the breaking of a horse. Any noise would distract the horse, and hours spent winning its confidence would be lost.

Dust settled gradually around them as they stood just inside the corral. There was no breeze now, and the heat was intolerable. Martin was drenched in perspiration, but it gave him no relief. The flies annoyed him, the dust choked him, and the sudden silence oppressed him. How did the mare stand it?

She stood for a moment, sniffing the air, sensing some difference and trying to understand what it might mean for her. She pivoted slowly, seeing first the wide pampa and then the people outside the corral and finally focusing on Martin and his uncle. Epifanio walked a few steps toward her. She caught his scent and shied. She gave a high, frightened whinny. Martin longed to answer as he often did in the pasture. His throat felt dry. She whinnied again and again, high, short, and ever more fearful cries now.

Suddenly she went wild, charging the corral at every point, her nostrils dilated with fury and fear, her long mane like a cloud and her tail held high and switching constantly. She snorted, charging both men and corral. Epifanio and Martin leaped through the blinding dust to the railing.

She galloped round and round the corral, no longer

with purpose but crazed with fear. Martin longed to comfort her. She seemed so alone, charging around without another of her kind, while the people stared at her.

An Indian brave trained his horse over a period of months without ever using a corral or a whip or a quirt. He never allowed another human being to watch. He was one with his horse.

Epifanio sat quietly on the railing, waiting. Finally the filly slowed and stood in the middle of the ring, so perfect an Arabian that Martin gasped. He had not realized how beautifully she stood; and even through the dust, the sun reflected on a magnificent golden chestnut coat. There was both fear and pride in her stance. She was waiting to see what fate had in store for her.

Epifanio eased himself from the railing. The mare lay back her ears and curled her lip. But she stayed her ground and let the man make the next move. He clucked his tongue against the roof of his mouth in a call she could understand, a gentle call. He cooed to the horse. He did not go closer, but waited to see if the mare might come to him.

They looked at each other, the man and the horse. It was a battle of wills, but in the end Epifanio coaxed her toward him. He placed a carrot between them on the dirt. With a toss of her delicate head she eased toward it, nudged it, and the carrot disappeared into her mouth in three bites. All the while Epifanio talked softly, telling her of the places they might go together, the strange sights they would see, the fresh winds they would feel, the fine colts she would surely bear, and of anything else that came into his mind. Martin smiled as his uncle described the morning's milking and the beauty of the dawn over the pampa.

A man coughed! The horse stiffened and laid back her ears. The fool! He could cough at home in bed if he had to. What would she do? She neighed, and Martin's horse, Gatito, answered her this time. Why had he not answered before? Martin did not know. She cocked her head. Epifanio cooed. She answered. Good, she was not frightened. It was all right.

What a beauty! Surely Don Jaime would keep her for the ranch if all went well this afternoon, if they did a good job. What a terrible crime it would be if this horse were ruined during the breaking. Martin felt sick. So much depended on how well Epifanio and he did, not only for themselves and Don Jaime but for the little chestnut mare as well. He felt he had never *really* known this before, though he had talked of the responsibility of the domador. He looked at his slender little uncle and saw that he realized exactly what was at stake. His hands were clenched and his face tortured as he cooed gently to the mare.

Now! Epifanio moved imperceptibly toward the horse.

She stood her ground. He held out his hand, and without moving her hoofs she leaned forward to sniff it. Her velvet lips fumbled, searching the palm and the fingers. She wanted to know Epifanio by his scent, and he was willing. There was not one false move from either man or horse; the feline grace of the one was answered with an equal fluid beauty by the other. They looked as though they were dancing. It was mesmerizing.

The crowd sighed. Fools! The mare shied and backed away a few steps. Epifanio seemed not to notice. He kept talking and did not move his hand until she nuzzled him again. She looked young to be broken. Only a two-year-old. They must be breaking her early because of the drought. Like the seeds and the meager crops, her breaking must come too soon because of the drought. Epifanio must be particularly careful not to break her gentle spirit, because she was so young. The fierce sun left nothing untouched.

Epifanio was telling the little mare now how he admired the set of her head and the luminescence of her eyes; that she would surely be the mother of champions, a noble horse fit to be the companion of brave gauchos. He patted her back, running his hand over her spine. She arched her neck in pleasure.

He held the bridle in his other hand, trailing the rope in the dirt. He lifted the bridle and slipped it over the golden mare's head in one effortless motion. There was no hurry nor importance given the motion, nor any break in the rhythm of his voice, and the horse scarcely seemed to notice.

The bit hung loose still, and Epifanio eased it into her mouth. She worked her mouth around the alien metal uncomfortably, twisting her jaws in an effort to spit it out. Still Epifanio talked with her, explaining why the bit was necessary and telling her that within a week she would not feel it. She looked at Epifanio reproachfully, whinnied, shied, but did not break loose and run. This was crucial. If a horse objected too strenuously to the bit, the rest of the breaking must be postponed.

She bared her lip and tried to bite. Epifanio stood quietly petting and talking with her. She did not like what had happened, but she was not going to break. Martin looked over at his friend Carlos and smiled. Carlos raised two fingers in a V for victory signal. Epifanio and the mare had passed the first crucial stage.

Epifanio held the bridle while another gaucho slipped in and shackled the mare. This was done within a few seconds, while the horse was still objecting to the bit and before she knew what was happening. Martin wanted to cry out that it wasn't necessary to shackle this gentle one. She could be saddled without the torture of being tied while the saddle was cinched on her back. The Indians didn't shackle their horses. But he knew he could not say anything.

Now Epifanio and the other cowboy virtually threw the saddle on her back. Martin looked full into the horror and betrayal in her eyes. How could they do it? How could Epifanio be so gentle and then betray her? She screamed and bit and tried to roll on the ground, but the men stayed with her and kept cinching the saddle. Within a minute it was secured.

"*Hola!* Remove the shackles," Epifanio called. Martin moved almost automatically to his horse. The ropes were cut, and the man rolled out of the way as the horse charged again in all directions. Many a man had lost his life in this job. Epifanio jumped to a top rung of the corral just beside the gate. He waited while the horse charged and Martin mounted his stallion, Gatito, just outside the corral.

"Open the gates!" As the mare raced through the gates to freedom, Epifanio jumped on her back. In that split second Epifanio proved, as he always did, that he was indeed a domador. His black stallion was saddled in case he missed and had to chase, but he did not miss.

They were off and Martin was right with them, pacing them pitch for pitch as they headed for the open prairie.

"*Caray!*" yelled the old domador at the top of his lungs. "Do your best, little horse" was what he meant. He did not begrudge her spirit and understood how she hated the saddle. This Martin knew. He also knew his uncle enjoyed the wild ride.

"Hear the crowd," Epifanio bellowed at Martin as they headed straight for the prairie. Dimly, as if from another world beyond the dust and the jerking zigzagging rearing boiling ferment, he heard the people cheering them on.

"They're just letting off steam," he yelled back, and he heard his uncle's laugh.

They headed straight for the open prairie at full gallop, the wild mare whinnying and Gatito answering her. Her mane flew; she carried her tail straight up and her eyes flared defiance. She had been tricked! The pampa was her home, and she would be rid of all encumbrances there. She would be free again!

She galloped effortlessly, her tail flying in the wind she created. Martin and Gatito forced themselves to keep up with her. Within a few minutes Martin felt as if he he had been galloping for hours. He'd never be able to keep it up.

But the mare and Epifanio looked as if they could go on rearing and running forever. They were a match for each other. They were nearing the brush now, dangerous land where horses and riders were torn by thorns and bushes and brambles and ripped by unexpected tall branches or spikes. Epifanio had warned him to ride low and protect his eyes. The horse was intelligent, he'd said, and knew this was the spot to throw an unsuspecting man and be on her way.

On they roared, covered by dust that swirled over their heads and obscured the bushes that tore their pants and ripped open their legs and caught in manes and eyes. Sage and cotton were sparse this year, and had more seeds and brambles than ever in an effort to reproduce themselves after a year of drought and uncertainty. Martin felt that he had personally encountered every thorn on the pampa. Would it never end? Wouldn't the sun set, ever?

The mare held to no pattern; there was no figuring her desperate charges first one and then another. Again and again and again. She was mad to be free. Epifanio was determined to train her. Martin admired both the mare and his uncle. How did they do it?

Round and round they tore through pampa grass and pampa brush, farther and farther from the corral and possible help. The dust rose until the whole sky looked yellow and Martin felt they were enclosed in one horrible cocoon. Men and horses dripped with sweat and were caked with dust.

How long had they ridden? Martin felt with every bone in his body that it had been forever.

Epifanio was singing. Singing! He was absolutely out of his mind.

Suddenly the mare tripped and fell. Epifanio was thrown. Martin lassoed the mare and pulled the rope taut. She would trample her rider if she got the chance.

Where was Epifanio? Over there. He seemed to be sitting up. He must be all right. Dimly Martin heard people yelling. They must have seen what had happened from the corral. They would send help.

Meanwhile the mare reared and kicked and pawed the air while Martin struggled desperately to keep the rope taut as Epifanio had shown him. He had to hold on. He had to keep hold of her until help came and his uncle was safely away. Martin no longer even thought of whether he was breaking the horse properly or breaking her at all. He was simply keeping her out of his uncle's way. Tears ran down his face, tears of frustration and fatigue and fear, but he held on. He didn't know where he was or even if he was tired. He simply *had* to keep hold of that rope! The rope and the dangerous wild horse were all the realities he knew.

So it was a surprise when he realized they were slowing down. He felt contrite when he saw that both the mare and Gatito were foaming at the mouth. Perhaps he was foaming, too. The wild horse slowed to a walk and stopped. Martin and Gatito stopped also. The ground reeled beneath them, and Martin felt he would fall. Just at this moment he saw that they were virtually surrounded by people. Everyone from the corral must be there. What business was it of theirs? They had not ridden.

"My uncle?" he asked.

"At your service, Segundo," Epifanio replied, and Martin realized he was standing beside him, offering to help him from his horse.

"Is it all right? Won't she run away?" he asked in a daze, pulling the rope taut.

Without a word Epifanio took the rope and walked toward the shivering horse. She did not move or shy. He motioned the onlookers to silence. Martin was stunned. What was Epifanio doing?

The man patted the wild mare. He told her again all the little flattering tales of what a great mother and companion she would become. He told her she had thrown him as no other horse had done in a dozen years. She should be proud and gracious to a man she had defeated so gallantly, he added softly. At first she shivered with fear and exhaustion, but gradually she responded to the man's gentle touch and finally nuzzled his hand, sniffing strangely at her own scent there.

Suddenly Epifanio leaped from the ground and onto her back in one fluid motion. She reared automatically and then frantically and finally desperately, but he hung on, yelling and encouraging her to do her best, for she would not throw Epifanio Guimenez twice in one afternoon. A few minutes later they were galloping in perfect unison and understanding, as if she had been Epifanio's mount for years.

Epifanio rode the mare back to the corral, leaped from

her back, and tied the reins to a post. He was peacefully currying her by the time the rest of the group trudged up.

"I have never seen anything like it," Don Jaime said, voicing everyone's opinion.

"Did I not say the boy would be tall indeed if trained by his uncle," the aunt reminded them as she puffed up.

"Your mare, Patrón," Epifanio said, bowing and handing the reins to Don Jaime, just as if this had been only one more breaking, just as the reins had been handed to the owner by the domador on the Roca Estancia for a hundred years.

"Thank you, Domador. I am in your debt," responded Don Jaime, accepting them.

The spectators clapped and yelled. This had been a doma to remember. Even Martin had never seen Epifanio or anyone else jump on a wild horse's back when the angry animal wore a saddle—and to jump from the ground without using the stirrups—well, it was fantastic!

"And the segundo who rode like a domador—hooray! Hooray!"

Martin blushed as he heard himself cheered. This had, after all, been Epifanio's day, and he was content that it was so. It was hard to understand, though, why Epifanio had not said one word of thanks for keeping the mare out of his way. He expected it, Martin realized suddenly. He expected it! So of course he would never compliment him. That was his uncle! What could you do with a man like that? Martin shook his head and hardly heard Carlos congratulating him.

"Bravo, bravo!" Carlos said.

"The new segundo will train this mare!" Don Jaime shouted above the general tumult. "And you and your uncle must come to the house where we can celebrate tonight," he added.

"Then we must rest before the fiesta," Epifanio said, turning to Martin for the first time since the wild mare had been tamed. "The sky is already red."

It was true. The sunset had thrown a band of scarlet across the sky that reflected back through the pampa so the entire land was red. But there was a coolness now that brought relief after the relentless day. As Martin and his uncle rode silently back across the wide plain to their one room *casita*, the boy felt the vastness of the land that stretched farther than he could see on every side, almost unbroken by houses or fences or trees. He thought of the old saying, "Man's work is no more than a grain of sand in the pampa." Still, what did it require to really please Epifanio? He, Martin, had spent his life trying to please this uncle who had reared him from babyhood, since the day his parents were killed in an automobile accident; and still he was no more than a grain of sand in the vastness of his uncle's thought. He usually satisfied him. Epifanio was rarely angry with him as he was with everyone else on the ranch. But he *never* complimented him. Martin felt he had done well today. Everyone else thought so. Why hadn't Epifanio? Was he clearing his throat to say something?

"Martin," the old domador began. "Martin, I do not want you to think I jumped on the wild mare's back just to show I could ride her. I did not know if I could do it or not, but if she were not broken today there would be no other chance, with all the horses to be broken before next market—because of the drought they must all be sold."

"Even this beauty—they can't!"

"Unless it rains they must."

Martin felt sick. They couldn't sell this horse. If it weren't for the drought they would not consider selling such a superior mare. He *had* to find a way to keep her.

"Martin," his uncle went on, "today, you did well." He said this last very shyly and with pride. But Martin was thinking of the mare and did not hear him. The old gaucho did not repeat what he had said.

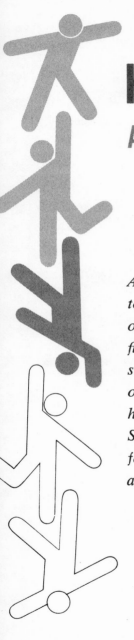

Hello, Aurora

ANNE-CATH. VESTLY

*Aurora and her family have just moved
to a new apartment house on the outskirts
of their Norwegian town; and Aurora is
finding it hard to make friends, especially
since her family seems different from
others she sees. But she enjoys helping
her father take care of her baby brother,
Socrates. Their trip to the baby clinic
for a checkup causes some comment,
and when they get home . . .*

Almost as High as the Sky

Luckily the elevator in Building Z was big. Aurora and Father pushed the baby carriage right inside it. The baby carriage would not have been easy to carry up the stairs because they had to go up to the tenth floor. Then they went down a long hall that had lots of doors all alike, but Aurora knew exactly which door was theirs. Father had made a beautiful nameplate which said: "Aurora, Marie, Edward, and Socrates Tege live here." Marie and Edward were Mother's and Father's names.

While Father put the kettle on and sewed the button on his coat, Aurora stood looking out of the window.

"Sometimes," she said, "it's just as if we had moved to America and were pioneers like the ones you told me about."

"Do you think so?" said Father. "But we don't have any land and we're not building a house, either."

"Yes, but it's just as if a lot of Indians were living in our building," said Aurora, "and they don't like our coming here because we didn't live here before. We're not welcome. Will I have to fight all the Indians?"

"Pioneers took the Indians' land, Aurora. We haven't taken anything from anyone. We've rented an apartment that was for rent. Why should you fight?"

"I think everybody fights in this building," said Aurora. "Maybe they don't have anything else to do. How is a baby like Socrates going to get along?"

"He doesn't need to worry," said Father. "He can lie in his blanket and look around him for a long time. You'll get to know everyone after a while. You'll find that a building like this is a world in itself. There are people here from all over the place. Some are nice, others have had such a bad time that they are hard to get along with; some wish they were back where they came from, others dream of living somewhere very different. They *all* have their own problems."

"Daddy," said Aurora, "can't you go out early in the morning and take a lunch bag with you and then sneak back later?"

"Why in the world should I do that?" asked Father.

"Well, because everybody asks why you are at home and don't work," said Aurora.

"Now wait a minute," said Father. "I'll just make the tea. We want plenty of time to talk about this. Take a look at Socrates and ask him nicely if he can wait until we've eaten."

Aurora crept into the bedroom. The baby carriage stood in front of the open window. Socrates was sleeping peacefully.

"It's all right," whispered Aurora when she came back again. "We can eat now."

Father had a lot of tea and a little milk, and Aurora had a little tea and a lot of milk. They both ate as if they hadn't seen food for a long time. Neither of them had had much appetite before going to the baby clinic.

"Now I'll tell you a thing or two," said Father. "If the other children here say I don't work, you can say: 'There are many ways of working and my father works in his own way.' When your Mother and I met each other we were both students. I was studying Greek and history and Mother was studying law. We decided to get married. Then we had you, and we couldn't leave you alone, could we? Mother was able to get a good job and earn a good salary, and I was able to work at home and try to earn something that is called a doctorate in history and also find time to practice the piano."

"And take care of us," said Aurora.

"Yes," said Father. "One of these days maybe *I* will be the one who goes out and it will be Mother who stays at home. But there's one thing I want to tell you: I think housework is fun. Mother doesn't think so. She has a very good brain and is very smart but her hands don't agree with one another when they have to do housework. Now, young lady, you can hold your head up and go out and tell anyone who asks that everybody is different. Some fathers work at home and some don't."

"Yes, I see," said Aurora. "But do I really have to go out?"

"Yes," said Father, "you have to get some fresh air, but you can wait until I've looked after Socrates if you want. You'll soon get to know some other little girls and boys."

Aurora and her father took the baby bottle out of the refrigerator and put it in hot water. Then Aurora went to get Socrates. She carried him in all by herself and put him on the table. Father changed him and said "bsbsbsbsbsbs" when Socrates didn't like lying on his back. As soon as he was turned over onto his tummy he was good-tempered again. He smiled and nodded his head and looked as if he would like to jump off the table.

He was very hungry and wanted to put everything within reach into his mouth, but he had to wait until Father had finished. Aurora was allowed to give him his bottle. She held him carefully in the crook of her arm. Even though she was not very big, Socrates felt that she was warm and safe, and he was very pleased that somebody had time to hold him while he was having his bottle. After he ate he had to be held against Father's shoulder to burp. Then he was put in his baby carriage out on the balcony. He fell asleep almost immediately.

Father said, "Well, Aurora, I've two hours now before I have to fix dinner." He got his books, and Aurora knew that she had to go out.

First, she went into the hall and looked out of the

window. Standing there seemed to be quite safe. She stood there for a long time and looked at the fir trees far below her. On the hill she saw a lot of children. They were as small as tiny ants. A woman came out of a door nearby. It might be better to move away. Otherwise the woman would ask why she was standing there. Then she might ask if her mother was at home. And then maybe she would ask whether her father had a job, and then she would pat Aurora's head and say "Poor little thing," or something.

Nobody had asked these questions where they lived before, because there the people knew Mother and Daddy and the kind of work they did. The woman went toward the elevator and Aurora went toward the stairs. She would rather go that way because it took so long to get to the bottom. She had to go down ten floors. That was a lot of stairs. Maybe it would take so long that she wouldn't get down before dinner time and would have to go right back up.

She went down one step—and then another one. The wall beside the stairs was rough and caught at her fingers when she drew them over it. She placed her foot carefully on the next step, trying to be quiet, and indeed she made very little noise. Once she tried stamping her feet. It had sounded very strange, and echoed a long way below her. No, she had better move stealthily. She remembered all the children who lived in the building, the ones she had called Indians. She hoped she wouldn't meet any of them now, for nobody was with her. Maybe it would be better to hurry, after all, for the staircase was narrow. She looked out of the window. Now she had come far enough to look right into the top of a fir tree. It wasn't a small tree either. What would it be like to be as tall as that tree? Well, she'd better get going now, down and down.

Then suddenly, between the fourth and fifth floors, a boy stood right in the middle of the stairs. He wasn't more than nine years old, but Aurora thought he looked big and very grim.

"What are you doing here?" said the boy.

"I live here," said Aurora.

"Which floor?" said the boy.

"The tenth," said Aurora. "Do you?"

"Huh!" said the boy. "Why don't you take the elevator? Afraid?"

"It has always been a bright spot in history when people have felt the need to explore the secrets of the universe," said Aurora, "and that is what I'm doing now."

It was a good thing Aurora had listened so well when Father was talking because for a minute the boy was so surprised he couldn't speak.

She began to go down the stairs again but she was not safe yet.

"Hey, what's your name?" said the boy. He leaned over the banister and looked down at her.

"Aurora," said Aurora.

"Is that your *name?*" said the boy.

"Yes, it is," said Aurora, "and it means something but I'm not going to tell you what."

"It doesn't mean anything," said the boy.

"Oh yes it does," said Aurora, "but I won't tell you because—because—"

She wanted to say that it was because he was rude, but she didn't dare. He was coming after her—no he wasn't, yes he was, no he wasn't . . . Aurora ran all the way down the stairs and outside. Her heart was beating fast because the boy had looked so frightening.

There were a lot of children outside the building. Some were playing and some were fighting and some were staring at Aurora. Aurora felt very small and lonely. She wanted to go back to her father, but that boy might still be standing on the stairs. She looked up at the windows. She looked and looked and was almost sure she could see where she lived. Why, there was Daddy standing up there and watching her. She waved with all her might. He waved back, but Aurora couldn't make him understand that she wanted him to come down and meet her so that she could get upstairs again

safely. She tried to signal "Come down" but he just nodded and went back to his work.

No, it was no use. He was up there, nearly as high as
the sky, and she stood down here on the ground unable
to shout because then everyone would hear her. It was
impossible. But she would do something else. She would
walk away from the building, a long, long way, for
Mother would be coming home again some time. She
would be so happy if Aurora came to meet her. It might
be a long time before she came, but that didn't matter.
Aurora set off. She walked quickly and hoped everyone
who saw her thought what a busy little girl she was.

Maybe they thought she was going to the supermarket.
There were plenty of interesting things to see in the store
windows. If only Socrates were a little bigger, he and
she would go there together. That would be fun. She
would hold his hand and they could talk to each other.
Oh, how she looked forward to his getting big enough
to walk or at least big enough to sit up in his baby carriage and look around him. She would show him everything: the houses and the trees and all the fascinating
things in the store windows. He didn't know much yet.
He just ate and slept and wet his diapers and that was
all. Still, he knew Mother and Daddy and her. He cried
when he saw strangers. So it was a good thing Daddy
was at home. Suppose she had to take care of him all
by herself. She might manage it, but she couldn't have

taken him to the clinic on her own; she and Daddy had to do that together.

Aurora stood in front of the supermarket for a long time and then she began to walk along the side of the road.

A few cars came by, but Mother wasn't in any of them. Aurora stood at the top of a long hill because there she could see all the cars that passed. She would know when Mother came because nobody else had a car like hers. Daddy had painted it last spring. It was blue with red fenders. Daddy had said that in a big town like Oslo so many people had cars that it might be hard to know which one was theirs. When Aurora was up on the tenth floor at home, she often looked down at their car. She could pick it out right away even though at least a hundred others were parked in rows in the parking lot.

Many cars came up the hill. There were a lot of women drivers. Sometimes only their heads could be seen above the steering wheels. They all looked rushed because it was nearly time to put the dinner on. The big trucks seemed to have more time to spare. It was too early for them to drive home so they climbed the hill slowly, making a terrific noise.

Mother was allowed to come home at about two-thirty—earlier than the others in the office because she had Socrates—and that was a good thing because she didn't have to drive during rush hour when everybody else who worked in town was going home too.

It was cold waiting. Aurora tried to stand on one leg at a time and warm the other foot against her calf, but it didn't help very much.

She closed her eyes and kept them shut for a long time; maybe when she opened them Mother would be there.

No, not yet. Maybe if she started to walk back, then she would hear the noise of a car and then maybe it would be Mother. But she barely would have time to wave. No, that wasn't a good idea either. It was better to go forward and keep looking. The light was beginning to fade on this winter afternoon; some of the cars had their lights on and the windows in the houses began to shine so that it looked even darker outside.

Aurora shut her eyes again. When she opened them it didn't seem quite so dark after all. And then she saw her mother's car chugging up the hill towards her. Aurora jumped up and down wildly. She took off her cap and waved it.

Luckily Mother saw her and stopped. "Why, it's my little girl! Have you come all this way to meet me?" she said.

"Yes," said Aurora. She crawled into the car beside her mother. It was nice and warm inside and it felt good just to sit down.

"Does Daddy know you're here?" asked Mother.

"No," said Aurora. "I couldn't tell him when he was up and I was down, because he couldn't hear me."

"Yes, but you could have gone up and asked him," said Mother.

"There was a boy on the stairs," said Aurora.

"I see," said Mother. "I'm glad I saw you. Are you terribly cold?"

"Not now," said Aurora. She sat there as pleased as she could be.

"It's good to be going home now. Maybe Daddy will have the dinner ready if he has had time," said Mother.

"We're going to have sausages and chocolate pudding," said Aurora. "You know that because you bought them yesterday."

"Yes," said Mother, "and today I bought ground beef for tomorrow. All the people in the stores we used to go to asked how you are, Aurora, and Mr. Larsen sent you some grapes."

"Oh," said Aurora. "I wish we could go to his store every day."

"Isn't it good to think how nice and warm it is at home?" said Mother. "In the old house we always had to build the fire up, didn't we?"

"Yes," said Aurora, "but it was cozy."

"Aurora," said Mother, "I won't ask you about the

day now, we'll wait until we get home to Daddy, but just tell me one thing. Did you manage all right with Socrates' shots? And what about Daddy?"

"It was fine," said Aurora. "Daddy didn't faint. They let me go in and hold Socrates."

"Smart girl," said Mother. "You and Daddy can tell me the rest together."

The journey home was almost too short, thought Aurora. She had walked a long way but it didn't seem long at all when she rode back. Mother parked the car and locked it. She took Aurora's hand and walked up to their building.

Aurora looked around her. There was that boy again. He was with some other boys and they were pushing and jostling each other. She thought she heard one of them say to him: "Are you coming out with us today, Knurre?"

"Don't know," said the boy who was called Knurre. Just as she and her mother went by, he said, "Au*ror*a." He didn't say any more, though, for Mother was there.

"Do you know some other children already?" asked Mother. "How nice."

They went up in the elevator and then they were home.

Father was in the kitchen. He had a book in one hand and a whisk in the other.

"Do you know, Aurora," he said, "I forgot that we were having chocolate pudding today, so now it's chocolate soup instead. Guess how good it is!"

"Chocolate soup?" said Mother in surprise. "I've certainly never tasted *that* before."

"Neither have I," said Father, "for I've just invented it, but it's wonderful. You make some white sauce and add cocoa and sugar and a little cooking chocolate. I did some spaghetti with the sausages, and we've got five potatoes left over from yesterday. Come and eat."

"Thank you very much," said Mother. "I'll just put the ground meat in the refrigerator."

Mother ate and yawned and ate again, and Father and Aurora told her all about their day and how well they had done at the clinic. Father changed Socrates and Mother fed him. Aurora and Father did the dishes. And then Mother, Father, and Socrates wanted their afternoon nap.

In the Middle of the Night

PHILIPPA PEARCE

In the middle of the night a fly woke Charlie. At first he lay listening, half-asleep, while it swooped about the room. Sometimes it was far; sometimes it was near—that was what had woken him; and occasionally it was very near indeed. It was very, very near when the buzzing stopped; the fly had alighted on his face. He jerked his head up; the fly buzzed off. Now he was really awake.

The fly buzzed widely about the room, but it was thinking of Charlie all the time. It swooped nearer and nearer. Nearer . . . .

Charlie pulled his head down under the bedclothes. All of him under the bedclothes, he was completely protected; but he could hear nothing except his heartbeats and his breathing. He was overwhelmed by the smell of warm bedding, warm pajamas, warm himself. He was going to suffocate. So he rose suddenly up out of the bedclothes; and the fly was waiting for him. It dashed at him. He beat at it with his hands. At the same time he appealed to his younger brother, Wilson, in the next bed: "Wilson, there's a fly!"

Wilson, unstirring, slept on.

Now Charlie and the fly were pitting their wits against each other: Charlie pouncing on the air where he thought the fly must be; the fly sliding under his guard toward his face. Again and again the fly reached Charlie; again and again, almost simultaneously, Charlie dislodged him. Once he hit the fly—or, at least, hit where the fly had been a second before, on the side of his head; the blow was so hard that his head sang with it afterward.

Then suddenly the fight was over; no more buzzing. His blows—or rather, one of them—must have told.

He laid his head back on the pillow, thinking of going to sleep again. But he was also thinking of the fly, and now he noticed a tickling in the ear he turned to the pillow.

It must be—it *was*—the fly.

He rose in such panic that the waking of Wilson really seemed to him a possible thing, and useful. He shook him repeatedly. "Wilson—Wilson, I tell you, there's a fly in my ear!"

Wilson groaned, turned over very slowly like a seal in water, and slept on.

The tickling in Charlie's ear continued. He could just imagine the fly struggling in some passageway too narrow for its wingspan. He longed to put his finger into his ear and rattle it around, like a stick in a rabbit hole; but he was afraid of driving the fly deeper into his ear.

Wilson slept on.

Charlie stood in the middle of the bedroom floor, quivering and trying to think. He needed to see down

59

his ear, or to get someone else to see down it. Wilson wouldn't do; perhaps Margaret would.

Margaret's room was next door. Charlie turned on the light as he entered: Margaret's bed was empty. He was startled, and then thought that she must have gone to the bathroom. But there was no light from there. He listened carefully: there was no sound from anywhere, except for the usual snuffling moans from the hall, where Floss slept and dreamed of dog biscuits. The empty bed was mystifying; but Charlie had his ear to worry about. It sounded as if there were a pigeon inside it now.

Wilson asleep; Margaret vanished; that left Alison. But Alison was bossy, just because she was the eldest; and anyway she would probably only wake Mum. He might as well wake Mum himself.

Down the passage and through the door always left ajar. "Mum," he said. She woke, or at least half-woke, at once. "Who is it? Who? Who? What's the matter? What?—"

"I've a fly in my ear."

"You can't have."

"It flew in."

She switched on the bedside light, and as she did so, Dad plunged beneath the bedclothes with an exclamation and lay still again.

Charlie knelt at his mother's side of the bed, and she looked into his ear. "There's nothing."

"Something crackles."

"It's wax in your ear."

"It tickles."

"There's no fly there. Go back to bed and stop imagining things."

His father's arm came up from below the bedclothes. The hand waved about, settled on the bedside light, and clicked it out. There was an upheaval of bedclothes and a comfortable grunt.

"Good night," said Mum from the darkness. She was already allowing herself to sink back into sleep again.

"Good night," Charlie said sadly. Then an idea occurred to him. He repeated his good night loudly and added some coughing, to cover the fact that he was closing the bedroom door behind him—the door that Mum kept open so that she could listen for her children. They had outgrown all that kind of attention, except possibly for Wilson. Charlie had shut the door against Mum's hearing because he intended to slip downstairs for a drink of water—well, for a drink and perhaps a snack. That fly business had woken him up and also weakened him; he needed something.

He crept downstairs, trusting to Floss's good sense not to make a row. He turned the foot of the staircase toward the kitchen, and there had not been the faintest whimper from her, far less a bark. He was passing the dog basket when he had the most unnerving sensation of something being wrong there—something unusual, at least. He could not have said whether he had heard something or smelled something—he could certainly have seen nothing in the blackness; perhaps some extra sense warned him.

"Floss?" he whispered, and there was the usual little scrabble and snuffle. He held out his fingers low down for Floss to lick. As she did not do so at once, he moved them towards her, met some obstruction—

"Don't poke your fingers in my eye!" a voice said, very low-toned and cross. Charlie's first, confused thought was that Floss had spoken: the voice was familiar—but then a voice from Floss should *not* be familiar; it should be strangely new to him—

He took an uncertain little step toward the voice, tripped over the obstruction, which was quite wrong in shape and size to be Floss, and sat down. Two things now happened. Floss, apparently having climbed over the obstruction, reached his lap and began to lick his face. At the same time a human hand fumbled over his face, among the slappings of Floss's tongue, and settled over his mouth. "Don't make a row! Keep quiet!" said the same voice. Charlie's mind cleared; he knew, although without understanding, that he was sitting on the floor in the dark with Floss on his knee and Margaret beside him.

Her hand came off his mouth.

"What are you doing here anyway, Charlie?"

"I like that! What about you? There was a fly in my ear."

"Go on!"

"There was."

"Why does that make you come downstairs?"

"I wanted a drink of water."

"There's water in the bathroom."

"Well, I'm a bit hungry."

"If Mum catches you. . . ."

"Look here," Charlie said, "you tell me what you're doing down here."

Margaret sighed. "Just sitting with Floss."

"You can't come down and just sit with Floss in the middle of the night."

"Yes, I can. I keep her company. Only at weekends, of course. No one seemed to realize what it was like for her when those puppies went. She just couldn't get to sleep for loneliness."

"But the last puppy went weeks ago. You haven't been keeping Floss company every Saturday night since then."

"Why not?"

Charlie gave up. "I'm going to get my food and drink," he said. He went into the kitchen, followed by Margaret, followed by Floss.

They all had a quick drink of water. Then Charlie and Margaret looked into the larder: the remains of a joint; a very large quantity of mashed potato; most of a loaf; eggs; butter; cheese . . .

"I suppose it'll have to be just bread and butter and a bit of cheese," said Charlie. "Else Mum might notice."

"Something hot," said Margaret. "I'm cold from sitting in the hall comforting Floss. I need hot cocoa, I think." She poured some milk into a saucepan and put it on the hot plate. Then she began a search for the cocoa. Charlie, standing by the cooker, was already absorbed in the making of a rough cheese sandwich.

The milk in the pan began to steam. Given time, it rose in the saucepan, peered over the top, and boiled over on to the hot plate, where it sizzled loudly. Margaret rushed back and pulled the saucepan to one side. "Well, really, Charlie! Now there's that awful smell! It'll still be here in the morning, too."

"Set the fan going," Charlie suggested.

The fan drew the smell from the cooker up and away through a pipe to the outside. It also made a loud roaring noise. Not loud enough to reach their parents, who slept on the other side of the house—that was all that Charlie and Margaret thought of.

Alison's bedroom, however, was immediately above the kitchen. Charlie was eating his bread and cheese, Margaret was drinking her cocoa, when the kitchen door opened and there stood Alison. Only Floss was pleased to see her.

"Well!" she said.

Charlie muttered something about a fly in his ear, but Margaret said nothing. Alison had caught them red-handed. She would call Mum downstairs, that was obvious. There would be an awful row.

Alison stood there. She liked commanding a situation.

Then, instead of taking a step backward to call up the stairs to Mum, she took a step forward into the kitchen. "What are you having, anyway?" she asked. She glanced with scorn at Charlie's poor piece of bread and cheese and at Margaret's cocoa. She moved over to the larder, flung open the door, and looked searchingly inside. In such a way must Napoleon have viewed a battlefield before the victory.

Her gaze fell upon the bowl of mashed potato. "I shall make potato cakes," said Alison.

They watched while she brought the mashed potato to the kitchen table. She switched on the oven, fetched her other ingredients, and began mixing.

"Mum'll notice if you take much of that potato," said Margaret.

But Alison thought big. "She may notice if some potato is missing," she agreed. "But if there's none at all, and if the bowl it was in is washed and dried and stacked away with the others, then she's going to think she must have made a mistake. There just can never have been any mashed potato."

Alison rolled out her mixture and cut it into cakes; then she set the cakes on a baking tin and put it in the oven.

Now she did the washing up. Throughout the time they were in the kitchen, Alison washed up and put away as she went along. She wanted no one's help. She was very methodical, and she did everything herself to be sure that nothing was left undone. In the morning there must be no trace left of the cooking in the middle of the night.

"And now," said Alison. "I think we should fetch Wilson."

The other two were aghast at the idea; but Alison was firm in her reasons. "It's better if we're all in this together, Wilson as well. Then, if the worst comes to the worst, it won't be just us three caught out, with Wilson hanging on to Mum's apron strings, smiling innocence. We'll all be for it together; and Mum'll be softer with us if we've got Wilson."

They saw that, at once. But Margaret still objected. "Wilson will tell. He just always tells everything. He can't help it."

Alison said, "He always tells everything. Right. We'll give him something *to* tell, and then see if Mum believes him. We'll do an entertainment for him. Get an umbrella from the hall and Wilson's sou'wester and a blanket or a rug or something. Go on."

They would not obey Alison's orders until they had heard her plan; then they did. They fetched the umbrella and the hat, and lastly they fetched Wilson, still sound asleep, slung between the two of them in his eiderdown. They propped him in a chair at the kitchen table, where he still slept.

By now the potato cakes were done. Alison took them out of the oven and set them on the table before Wilson. She buttered them, handing them in turn to Charlie and Margaret and helping herself. One was set aside to cool for Floss.

The smell of fresh-cooked, buttery potato cake woke Wilson, as was to be expected. First his nose sipped the air; then his eyes opened; his gaze settled on the potato cakes.

"Like one?" Alison asked.

Wilson opened his mouth wide, and Alison put a potato cake inside, whole.

"They're paradise cakes," Alison said.

"Potato cakes?" said Wilson, recognizing the taste.

"No, paradise cakes, Wilson," and then, stepping aside, she gave him a clear view of Charlie's and Margaret's entertainment, with the umbrella and the sou'wester hat and his eiderdown. "Look, Wilson, look."

Wilson watched with wide-open eyes, and into his

wide-open mouth Alison put, one by one, the potato cakes that were his share.

But, as they had foreseen, Wilson did not stay awake for very long. When there were no more potato cakes, he yawned, drowsed, and suddenly was deeply asleep. Charlie and Margaret put him back into his eiderdown and took him upstairs to bed again. They came down to return the umbrella and the sou'wester to their proper places, and to see Floss back into her basket. Alison, last out of the kitchen, made sure that everything was in its place.

The next morning Mum was down first. On Sunday she always cooked a proper breakfast for anyone there in time. Dad was always there in time; but this morning Mum was still looking for a bowl of mashed potato when he appeared.

"I can't think where it's gone," she said. "I can't think."

"I'll have the bacon and eggs without the potato," said Dad; and he did. While he ate, Mum went back to searching.

Wilson came down, and was sent upstairs again to put on a dressing gown. On his return he said that Charlie was still asleep and there was no sound from the girls' rooms either. He said he thought they were tired out. He went on talking while he ate his breakfast. Dad was reading the paper and Mum had gone back to poking about in the larder for the bowl of mashed potato, but Wilson liked talking even if no one would listen. When Mum came out of the larder for a moment, still without her potato, Wilson was saying: ". . . and Charlie sat in an umbrella boat on an eiderdown sea, and Margaret pretended to be a sea serpent, and Alison gave us paradise cakes to eat. Floss had one too, but it was too hot for her. What are paradise cakes? Dad, what's a paradise cake?"

"Don't know," said Dad, reading.

"Mum, what's a paradise cake?"

"Oh, Wilson, don't bother so when I'm looking for something. . . . When did you eat this cake, anyway?"

"I told you. Charlie sat in his umbrella boat on an eiderdown sea and Margaret was a sea serpent and Alison—"

"Wilson," said his mother, "you've been dreaming."

"No, really—really!" Wilson cried.

But his mother paid no further attention. "I give up," she said. "That mashed potato; it must have been last weekend. . . ." She went out of the kitchen to call the others. "Charlie! Margaret! Alison!"

Wilson, in the kitchen, said to his father, "I wasn't dreaming. And Charlie said there was a fly in his ear."

Dad had been quarter-listening; now he put down his paper. "What?"

"Charlie had a fly in his ear."

Dad stared at Wilson. "And what did you say that Alison fed you with?"

"Paradise cakes. She'd just made them, I think, in the middle of the night."

"What were they like?"

"Lovely. Hot, with butter. Lovely."

"But were they—well, could they have had any mashed potato in them, for instance?"

In the hall Mum was finishing her calling. "Charlie! Margaret! Alison! I warn you now!"

"I don't know about that," Wilson said. "They were paradise cakes. They tasted a bit like the potato cakes Mum makes, but Alison said they weren't. She specially said they were paradise cakes."

Dad nodded. "You've finished your breakfast. Go up and get dressed, and you can take this"—he took a coin from his pocket—"straight off to the sweetshop. Go on."

Mum met Wilson at the kitchen door. "Where's he off to in such a hurry?"

"I gave him something to buy sweets with," said Dad. "I wanted a quiet breakfast. He talks too much."

Shurik:
A Story of the
Siege of Leningrad

KYRA PETROVSKYA WAYNE

There has never been such a cold winter before, I thought as I trotted down the middle of the icy street. The soles of my military boots thumped against snow packed hard as stone, creating a feeling of "pins and needles" in my frozen toes. The sensation was almost pleasant, for it made me feel warmer.

I thought with longing of my cozy room a short distance away. In a few minutes I would start a fire in my ceramic stove with the shelves from my bookcase. The shelves were made of stained mahogany, dry, and heavy. They would keep me warm for a while.

In the distance I heard the explosion of an artillery shell. It was another of the shells that had fallen upon Leningrad at random, for more than three months. Day and night one heard the deep, booming explosions, which spared no part of the city.

One more turn and I'll be home, I thought. I was ravenously hungry. I had been on duty for twelve hours and had eaten my daily bowl of soup standing up, at the nurses' station. I was tired, too. The Military Hospital No. 902—housed in a modern school building where I worked as a nurse—overflowed with wounded soldiers who kept arriving daily in great convoys of camouflaged trucks. At times we had to leave the soldiers in the trucks for a full day before beds became available in the hospital. We would give the men first aid and cover them with all the blankets we could spare, hoping that none would freeze to death before we could bring them inside. Some did freeze. . . .

A few more buildings to pass and I would be home. Home, until tomorrow, in the warmth of my own little room, baking potatoes in the hot coals of my stove, reading Hemingway in the flickering light of a candle. If I were lucky, there might be an hour or two of electric light. One never knew.

One more apartment house to pass or, rather, the ruins of a house. It had been hit by a shell only two days before. It must have been a huge shell, for the whole building had been destroyed. The explosion had shaken the entire neighborhood, shattering some windows in my apartment house and breaking my set of crystal glasses. Fortunately the windows in my room remained intact. Once broken, they could not be replaced.

As I passed the house, I looked at it again. My school friend, Nadya, used to live there. I wondered where she was now. Probably somewhere at the front. The last time I had seen her was during the summer, when we both were graduating from a *druzhinniza* class. She looked smart in her uniform with the field-nurse arm band and medical corps emblem on her military cap.

Once I was envious of her. She had been assigned to

front-line duty immediately, while I had been detained to take an additional course to become a hospital nurse. I wanted to go to the front. All my friends were there, fighting. And I felt that by staying behind and studying at the school of nursing, I was betraying my country. While my friends were constantly risking their lives, I learned to take the pulse and give an enema! But that was during the first months of the war, before Leningrad came under siege. Now, in November, the very streets of the city became the front lines. The bombardment of the city never stopped. Our patients at the hospital were only half joking when they complained that they felt safer at the front-line positions. There, at least, they could hide in their foxholes and wait until the worst was over. In the city they felt trapped behind the thin walls of the hospital. The shriek of bombs and the sound of long-range guns deprived our patients of sleep and made them nervous and restless.

I glanced at the demolished house again. There were four stories of apartments, neatly sliced in half like a dollhouse. I could see the remaining half of the rooms, as if they were part of a stage set. There were curtains on one window, and someone's coat on a nail gently swayed in the wind. In another room a baby grand piano stood precariously in a corner.

Something attracted my attention to a pile of brick

rubble at the foot of the bombed house. I thought I saw some movement. It was always possible that the Civil Defense Corps, which searched in the tumbled ruins for survivors, had overlooked someone. There were so many ruins, so many victims. I climbed over the pile of bricks, slippery under the freshly fallen snow.

"Anybody there?" I called.

"Yes. It's me, Shurik." A child's voice came faintly from the rubble in the depths of the shell crater.

"Are you hurt?" I cried.

"I'm so cold" was the reply. There was scratching and puffing, and in a few moments a small, dirty figure covered with powdery red-brick dust stood in front of me.

"Who are you? What's your name?" I asked.

"Shurik Nikanorov," replied the boy. He couldn't have been more than ten.

"What were you doing there?"

"I used to live there."

"But what were you doing there just now?" I insisted.

"I was looking for my mother. She must be there—somewhere. She was home when the house was hit. She must be there. Maybe she was in the shelter. I must find her," the boy babbled, as if in delirium.

I took his thin wrist in my hand and felt his pulse. It raced wildly. The child was feverish.

"Come with me," I said. "It's getting too dark to see

anything now. We'll look for your mother in the morning." Obediently Shurik put his cold, clawlike hand into mine.

"Here, put these on." I took my mittens off and handed them to Shurik. He tried to put them on, but his frozen fingers didn't obey him. He dropped the mittens.

"Let me help you," I said. One glance at the ruined building was enough to tell me that his mother must have been killed or wounded during the bombing. The civil defense workers had probably removed her body, either to a hospital or to a morgue.

"Where is your father?"

"At the front. He is a sergeant. A gunner in a tank battalion," Shurik answered, his teeth chattering.

"Do you have any other family? Grandparents, perhaps, or brothers or sisters?"

"No. My mother told me that I would have a little brother or sister in February."

Poor woman, I thought. My hands felt cold without mittens, but I couldn't release Shurik. Half supporting him with one hand, I stuck the other inside my military overcoat in Napoleonlike fashion, opening and closing my fingers to keep the circulation going.

"Just a few more steps," I said, mostly for my own benefit. Shurik was silent. He followed me trustingly, as if he had known me all his life.

"Here we are. Now, I must light a match so we won't

stumble in the dark." The matches were damp and refused to burn. I broke several before I was able to light one, which sputtered and crackled and promptly went out. But these scant seconds of light were enough to see a corpse, lying at the foot of the steps. *Another one*, I thought, as Shurik and I stepped over it and began our ascent to my flat on the fourth floor. This was the third body I had seen at the foot of the stairs within the week. In the morning—hopefully—it would be gone. The civil defense workers would remove it for burial.

I fumbled for my key and opened the door of my apartment. It was almost as cold as outdoors. We staggered in the dark through a communal kitchen, once filled with the laughter of the housewives who shared it. Now it was deserted. Most of the tenants had been mobilized into defense units, and those who remained huddled in their own rooms, preferring to cook their scanty meals on their own stoves like I did, guarding their precious food supplies from one another.

We stopped in front of my door. With another key, I opened a heavy padlock. At one time I left my room unlocked. Now it was impossible. My food, my wood, my water supply—everything would surely be stolen by my desperate neighbors.

It was warmer in my room. The embers in my ceramic stove still glowed a bit.

"Don't take your coat off until I start the fire," I said

to Shurik. "Sit down." Passively he sank to the floor from exactly where he was standing. I stumbled in the dark until I found a candle and a box of good, pre-war matches. The flickering candlelight made the room seem more cheerful.

"Sit on the sofa," I said to Shurik. "It's less cold there." Like a little robot he changed his place. I used pages from the *Great Soviet Atlas* to kindle the fire. This volume had seen me through many years at school, and now it helped me to survive my nineteenth year of life. On top of the paper went my bookshelves. The shelves caught at once. Next, the case itself would have to be burned, board by board, molding by molding.

I turned to Shurik. He was covered with brick dust from head to foot. I couldn't see his face, only two bright, feverish eyes.

"While our potatoes roast, I'll clean you up. You look like a red Indian." I tried to make him smile, but he merely stared.

I turned back to the stove and made a hollow in the coals under the grate and buried four potatoes there. "All right," I said, "soon our supper will be ready." I took my overcoat off and rolled up the sleeves of my military tunic.

"Now, Shurik, let me see your face. Take your hat off." He took his warm, fur-flapped hat off. His hair—

pale-blond, matted and in need of combing—looked like
a wig stuck on a red-faced mannequin.

"I don't have much water. We must save it for drinking. But, fortunately, I have a whole jar of vaseline.
We'll remove all this dirt just like actors do when they
remove their make-up," I said, reaching into my dressing
table for vaseline and cotton. Shurik waited, listlessly. I
took his dirty clothes off and wrapped him in my old
terry-cloth bathrobe. He shivered.

"Sit here, by the fire." I moved a chair in front of the
open door of the stove. The heat came out in waves, and
the room began to feel warm.

"Close your eyes and don't open them until I say so.
We don't want vaseline in your eyes," I said, beginning
the painstaking job of cleaning him up. Oh, to have a
bathtub, full of hot, soapy water!

"Where were you when the house was bombed?" I
asked casually. "Keep your eyes shut!"

"I was at the river, with my sled. Mother had sent me
for water."

How well I knew the task! All the pipes in the city
were solidly frozen. Everyone had to get their water from
the river. There were always crowds of women and children with their sleds and containers, waiting beside holes
in the ice to take turns dipping the muddy water. It was
a slippery, dangerous job.

"So?" I prompted Shurik to continue.

"So, I came home—and the house was gone. There were people and firemen yelling and running around. I got scared. I ran away. Later, when the firemen were gone, I returned and started searching for my mother."

"But the house was bombed two days ago!" I cried. "You mean you were there all that time? Even at night?"

"I guess so," Shurik whispered. "I didn't want to go until I found her."

Tears welled up in my eyes. I hugged Shurik tightly.

"We'll look for her tomorrow. I promise. I'm sure that the firemen would know where she is."

The room began to smell of the delicious roasting potatoes.

"Have you eaten anything during these two days?" I asked.

"Yes, I found an apple."

"And was that all?"

"Yes."

The water in my fire-blackened teapot began to boil and splatter on the coals. I pulled my mittens on and quickly drew the teapot out of the stove.

"In a few more minutes we'll have nice, hot tea. I even have a piece of sugar!" I said brightly.

Shurik's face, neck and hands were shiny with vaseline. They were finally clean of brick dust and grime. I combed his hair and lifted his pinched little face toward me. He was a beautiful child, blue-eyed and blond with thin, transparent skin. He sat shivering in front of the open stove, patiently waiting for me to give him something to eat.

I dug the black, cracked potatoes out of the coals. While they were cooling, I unlocked my jewelry case. Inside, wrapped carefully in a clean handkerchief, was a sizable lump of sugar. I had been saving it for New Year's Eve.

"Here," I said, "it's all for you!" I handed Shurik the sugar. He took it without enthusiasm. I felt disappointed. I had expected to see his face light up, but then I realized how sick he was. I touched his forehead. It was hot and dry. I felt his pulse. It was racing. He had a high fever. *I must get him to bed quickly*, I thought.

I poured hot tea into two cups and mashed Shurik's potatoes. I had no butter but lots of salt—plenty of coarse, grainy, dirty-looking salt. I remembered how, before the war, our janitor used to sprinkle the same kind of salt on the sidewalks during the winter to melt the snow. Now we were happy to eat it. How things had changed in a year!

Shurik ate his potatoes greedily.

Thank God, he still has an appetite. He can't be too sick then, I thought with relief.

We drank our tea and finished the potatoes. We used torn pages from the atlas as plates, for there was not enough water to spare for washing dishes. The glossy pages, wiped clean, could be used again until, finally, they would be good only for lighting the fire.

The room felt warm and cozy. I was drowsy with fatigue.

"Let's go to sleep. I'll fix the sofa for you. Take this aspirin." I tucked him under a blanket on the sofa. For good measure, I put my coat over him. Then I blew the candle out. My own bed felt icy, but I knew that soon I wouldn't notice it. I would be fast asleep. Even the constant boom of the artillery barrage would not disturb me.

I awakened with a start. Shurik was restless. He tossed and thrashed about in bed, mumbling deliriously. I touched his forehead. It was still burning. Toward the morning, Shurik's fever seemed to subside. He opened his eyes and smiled faintly at me. I was glad that he recognized me and wasn't afraid.

"Listen, Shurik," I said seriously. "I must go to work now, but you stay here until I come back. You're ill, so you must stay in bed. We'll search for your mother as soon as you get better. Meanwhile, I'll ask whether the civil defense people know where your mother is. One thing you must realize: she is *not* at the bombed house. Perhaps she is in some hospital."

"No," Shurik said faintly. "She is not in the hospital.

She is dead." I felt a chill run down my spine.

"Why do you say that?"

"I just know." There was resignation in his voice. It pained me to hear it.

"Nonsense!" I exclaimed. "Until we check the hospitals, we can't be sure of anything!"

"I just know," Shurik repeated and closed his eyes.

"Listen, Shurik, listen to my instructions. I'll light the stove now, so you won't be cold while I'm gone. Here is a slice of bread. Don't eat it all at once, even if you're very hungry. I'll cut it in three portions; eat only one piece at a time. One now, with tea; another, about noon; and the third when daylight begins to fade—about four-thirty or five. Soon after that I'll be home with more food."

Shurik nodded gravely.

I poured a cup of tea for Shurik and lifted him to a sitting position. *Too bad the sugar is gone*, I thought, as I held the cup to his lips. Shurik took two sips and fell back on the pillows.

"I'll drink it later," he murmured. I stood there, watching him. He seemed to drift into sleep again. He was breathing evenly, his forehead glistening with perspiration.

I wish I didn't have to go, I thought, as I buckled my heavy automatic service pistol to my belt. Then, glancing at Shurik once again to make sure he was asleep, I left the room.

"Lieutenant Petrovskaya, you're five minutes late!" said the chief of the hospital as I hurriedly put my hospital attire over my military uniform. The pistol was in my way, but it was against regulations for an officer to be without his weapon even for a few hours.

"I'm sorry, Colonel Stern. I had an unexpected complication at home," I apologized. I had never been late before, and I hoped that Dr. Stern would be lenient.

He peered at me over his glasses. "What kind of complication?" The doctor was wiping his hands meticulously with rubbing alcohol, for even at the hospital we had to preserve water.

"Yesterday I found an orphan, a small boy, sick and alone. I took him in—at least until he is well." The chief looked at me owlishly over the gold rims of his glasses. His bushy eyebrows were drawn into one straight line over his old wrinkled face.

"I hope you know what you're doing. It is impossible for you to keep the child," he said, reading my inner thoughts.

"Oh, I know, Comrade Colonel, I know. But I won't keep him longer than necessary—a day or two at the most. Then I'll notify the civil defense authorities. They might want to evacuate him from the city."

"See that you do." He looked at me shrewdly. "I know it is hard, but you cannot keep him."

How did he guess that I would like to keep Shurik? My chief never ceased to surprise me with his astuteness. . . .

I tied my white hospital smock at the back and hid my hair under a white cap. Then, washing my hands with alcohol, I followed Dr. Stern into the operating room. . . .

At noon we were finished. The second phase of our work at the hospital was about to begin—the treatment of the less seriously wounded in the wards. . . .

After our work in the wards, we all went downstairs to admit new patients who were to arrive momentarily. Only ward-duty nurses were excused from working in admissions; they were needed in the wards, one nurse for every twenty patients. . . .

It was always bedlam in the reception hall. We had several long tables lined up against the walls where receptionists wrote down administrative details about each patient. We, the nurses, were to provide first aid. When we had hot water, each patient was thoroughly washed, for everyone coming from the front was badly infested with lice.

Dr. Stern made a quick evaluation of each soldier's condition and gave orders for his placement in the wards.

Each convoy of wounded was accompanied by several

field nurses—*druzhinnizi*—who wore automatic subma-
chine guns negligently slung around their necks. Many
times the girls had to use those guns to fight off enemy
snipers who shot at them while they were trying to reach
the wounded men. These tough *druzhinnizi* used to look
at us, the hospital nurses, as if we were of a lower order.
What did we know of *real* danger, the *real* war fought
in the trenches? Had we ever seen a tank attack? Had we
ever been shot at? To them, we were pampered city girls,
well-educated and clever enough to escape *real* service by
flaunting our college degrees. They all but accused us
of cowardice.

But that was before the siege was tightened about the
city. Lately the attitude of the *druzhinnizi* toward the
hospital nurses began to change. Each time the rough
front-line girls arrived in the city with their convoy of
wounded soldiers, they saw the corpses lying in the streets,
frozen in the snow. They knew they had been victims of
starvation. The girls heard the never-ending bombardment and saw the devastation of one of the most beautiful cities in the world. Slowly they began to show signs
of compassion and sympathy for those of us who had to
remain at our posts in the stranded city. At the front at
least there was plenty of food, while in the city all of us,
young and old, were slowly starving to death.

The girls from the front began to show their friendship
by sharing their own food rations with us. Each time
they came to Leningrad, they brought us cans of meat

or fish, half-melted bars of chocolate which tasted like soap, lumps of gray sugar or a few raw potatoes. The sugar which I had given to Shurik was a gift from my front-line friend Valya.

She was a powerful peasant girl who could easily lift a grown man and carry him into the reception room. Valya once had seen me on the stage, just before the war. She recognized me now, in spite of my military uniform. It thrilled her that she knew a "real actress." She immediately became my friend. She worried about my sick pallor and loss of weight. I was sure that she committed a few acts of petty larceny to supply me with soap and sugar. I could give her nothing in return. I couldn't even invite her to stay with me during her trips to Leningrad. Valya had to return to the front immediately after her patients were admitted into the hospital. I felt embarrassed by accepting her gifts, but Valya only laughed. . . .

"Where is Lieutenant Petrovskaya?" demanded someone in a loud voice. A large, powerful-looking older woman wearing the uniform of a captain came toward me.

I saluted. She wearily motioned with her hand as if brushing a fly away, instead of a crisp military salute.

"At ease. I have a parcel for you from Valya Orlova. She couldn't come. She was wounded, but she wanted you to have this." The captain, the commander of the company, handed me a small package.

"Thank you, Comrade Captain. How is Valya?" I asked anxiously.

"She'll be all right soon. Nothing serious," she said offhandedly. Then, looking at the girls gathered around me, she commanded them to return to the trucks. I barely had time to wave good-by to my new friends and to thank the captain for Valya's present before the trucks roared off to the front for a new load of wounded.

I had no time to look at Valya's package, but I knew it was food.

"Hurry, comrades, hurry!" I heard the voice of Dr. Stern as he entered the reception room. "Soon it will be too dark to process the patients. I have just been informed that we ran out of candles!" He swore mightily. Some of the girls giggled. It was so funny to hear our gentle, dignified doctor using truck drivers' expressions. Somehow, on his lips, Russian curses lacked conviction.

We worked fast. There was just about an hour of daylight left. If we didn't process all the newly arrived men, we would have to leave them on the stretchers until next day. Without the candles our entire night crew would have to work by the light of a few flashlights— not an easy task in a hospital crowded with more than 700 patients. . . .

When I finally returned home and opened the padlock, I found Shurik asleep. The bread remained untouched, dried and shriveled now, but the tea was gone. I moved about the room, as quietly as possible, lighting the stove once more. I thought with dread of the necessity to trek to the river. It had to be done. I had no water left.

Shurik stirred, then opened his eyes. They were dull and vacant.

"Good evening, Shurik!" I said softly. "How do you feel?"

He looked at me for a few moments, as if not recognizing me. Then he attempted to smile.

"Awful," he said. "My bones hurt . . . and my head . . . and even my eyes," he said with effort.

I touched his forehead and took his pulse. He was still feverish.

"I brought you a real surprise," I said. "Just look at this!" I opened Valya's little parcel and brought its contents for Shurik to see. He glanced with indifference at our riches—two thick slices of smoked salami, one raw onion, two sections of a chocolate bar and a handful of broken hard candy.

"Look at all these sweets!" I exclaimed. But Shurik remained apathetic.

I sat next to him on the edge of the sofa. "Listen. I must go to the river now. Sleep until I get back. Then we'll have a little feast, all right?" He nodded, silently.

I hated to leave the room. The stove emitted wonderful warmth, the spicy smell of the salami was most enticing.

Maybe we can manage without water. Maybe there is enough snow on the window ledge outside which I might melt. I opened the small windowpane used for ventilation and peered outside. No. There was nothing left. I had forgotten that only yesterday I had scraped all the fresh snow to make a cup of tea. No, I must go to the river. I dressed again, but instead of my military cap, I draped a thick woolen shawl over my head and shoulders, completely hiding my military insignia. I stuck my automatic pistol into the pocket of my overcoat; it was dangerous to walk to the river at night. It was rumored that there were bands of thieves who would murder anyone for a pair of good boots or a book of ration coupons. Usually I would not go to the river at night; even the thought of it sent shivers down my spine.

In the daytime it was different. There was safety in the numbers of people at the river. However, at this hour, there would be no one. . . .

Once on the ice, I made my way to the nearest *prorub*, a hole, from which I would haul my water. I tied the rope to one of the buckets and lowered it into the *prorub*. I heard a splash as the bucket hit the water, and then I felt the rope tighten as it began to fill up. As soon as I felt its full weight, I pulled it up. . . .

The trek back was laboriously tortuous. I could not pull my heavily laden sled up the slippery steps. I had to carry each container separately and, once on the street again, reassemble them on the sled, tying them one to another. Then, pulling the sled behind me, I turned toward home.

The empty wide street, silvery under the moon, lay ahead of me. I walked slowly, trying not to spill any more of my precious cargo, watching for deep ruts in the snow which could overturn my clumsy sled and make my trip to the river all for naught. The rope from the sled cut into my hand, even through my mittens. I had to change hands often to reduce the pain.

The last ordeal awaited me at home. I had to make several trips up and down the staircase, for I could carry only two containers at a time. With my last trip, I brought my sled up and stored it under the bed once again. I had enough water now to last for three days!

Shurik was still sleeping. The room was very warm. There was enough fire in the stove to begin the next phase in making the water potable. It was a tedious but necessary process. The water, drawn from the river, was polluted and needed to be boiled and strained twice before it was safe for drinking. Even after this it still had a muddy color, but at least it was no longer contaminated.

I thought of boiling just enough water for tomorrow morning. I was too tired. But the thought that Shurik might use the polluted water in my absence made me work until two in the morning, until the last container of water had been purified.

Shurik slept throughout the whole procedure. I thought of awakening him and forcing him to eat, but I changed my mind. *Let him rest*, I thought. *It's probably best for him now.*

. . . *It's all for the best*, I thought. *Soon it will be morning, and we'll have Valya's salami for breakfast.* I undressed and went to bed. I had only four hours to sleep. I could not waste even one minute of it.

"How do you feel this morning?" I asked Shurik.

"I don't know . . . I feel very dizzy," he said in a hoarse voice. Then his thin body shook with paroxysms of heavy, dry painful coughs that left him exhausted. I supported his chest with my hands, trying to reduce his pain. He looked at me, his eyes slowly filling with tears.

"It hurts," he finally said, touching his chest. "It hurts all over."

"I know, I know. I'll bring a doctor later, and he'll give you something to make you better." Even as I said the words, I knew I was foolish. There were no doctors to take care of civilians. But I continued to stroke him, murmuring encouraging words, hoping that his coughing seizure would not return. He felt limp in my arms. His body was so thin that it seemed I could feel his every bone.

"Lie down, darling, keep warm. I must light the stove again." Obediently Shurik fell back on his pillows. He watched me as I prepared our breakfast, but his eyes were dull.

"Here we are. Breakfast is ready!" I announced cheerfully as I spread a tablecloth on the little table in front of the sofa. I didn't feel like eating off the *Great Soviet Atlas* this morning. Valya's generous present required a more elaborate setting.

Shurik didn't stir.

"You must eat a little," I said. "You haven't eaten anything for more than thirty-six hours or maybe longer. You're the world champion of noneaters!" A slow smile spread across his thin face. He pulled his right arm from under the blanket and squeezed his hand into a fist.

"I'm the champion!" he declared hoarsely, holding his fist up, like a boxer.

He can't be too sick if he can still joke! I thought with relief.

I propped Shurik up with pillows. He looked like a pitiful little chick, his neck thin and long, his blond hair ruffled and moist. He drank his tea and sucked on a candy. I made him swallow a few bites of bread and salami, but I could see that he did it only to please me. It was time for me to leave. As I was buttoning my coat he beckoned me to come closer to him.

"What is it?"

"I love you," he said as his thin arms encircled my neck and his cracked, dry lips touched my cheek. "Please, don't send me to an orphanage."

"Don't worry. Rest now," I said, but I knew that I

could not turn him over to the authorities. I didn't know how I was going to manage, but I was not going to send him away.

"Can you spare me one minute, Dr. Stern?" I asked as I knocked at the open door of his office.

"Come in," he said. "How is your foundling?"

"Oh, Dr. Stern, he is ill. He might even have pneumonia. He is so pitiful." In spite of my resolution to be brisk and professional, I began to cry.

"No, no, no. Don't do that. I can't stand women crying." Dr. Stern fussed over me, wiping my face with the skirt of his hospital coat. "I told you you should have taken him to the orphanage at once. Now it's too late, I know. You love him as if he were your own, no?"

I could only nod my head.

He walked to the window and stood there for a few seconds, his back toward me. "I'll tell you what you must do. Since you chose to keep him, you must take the full responsibility for his welfare." He pointed his finger at me as if assigning me to this special duty. "Now I'll help you as much as I can. I'll split your shifts into two six-hour segments. It means, of course, that you'll have to come to the hospital twice a day, but you live nearby. Next, I'll make a personal visit to your—what's his name?"

"Shurik. Shurik Nikanorov."

"I'll see your Shurik, right after our morning treatments. I have a few medications here which we can spare."

"Thank you. Thank you, Dr. Stern!" I said, overcome by the way he had read my thoughts. He waived my thanks impatiently.

"This is all I need. A pediatrics case! I haven't seen a sick child in fifty years!" he grumbled, pretending anger. "What do you feed him?" he demanded.

"Tea, bread and salami."

"Tea, bread and salami," he mimicked. "What kind of a diet is that for a sick child?"

I began to cry again. "But I don't have anything else!"

"Stop. Stop crying at once!" He hurried to dry my tears. "We'll do something . . . I'll bring a bit of oatmeal and a can or two of condensed milk. We can't let the child starve just because it's against the regulations to take food out of the hospital. But stop crying, for God's sake!" He walked to the window again and stood there, examining the frost designs on the windowpane.

"Does he have fever?"

"Yes, doctor. He has high fever. For two days now. And he sweats. And he has a bad, hacking cough."

"I don't like it. You're probably right. He may have pneumonia. I'll see him today, I promise. Now run along. I must scrub for surgery." I left his office, feeling elated. . . .

The air was fresh and frosty. For the second day now we had bright sunshine, so unusual in Leningrad during the winter. Dr. Stern and I walked briskly toward my house. Our deep pockets were bulging with canned milk, packages of oatmeal and even a small sack of sugar. Dr. Stern forbade me to inquire where he got the food. . . .

"Here is Shurik's house—or, rather what's left of it," I said as we passed the bombed building. Dr. Stern barely glanced at the house. His face was dark and sad. He was tired and sick at heart for his torn city.

"And here is my house. I live on the fourth floor. The stairs are steep, so let's preserve our strength." He gave me a sidelong glance.

"Are you implying that I'm old and decrepit? That I can't climb four flights of stairs without collapsing?" Then he smiled. "Well, you're right! I might collapse if we don't stop on every landing for a few moments. I have a bad heart." I wanted to say something sympathetic but Dr. Stern had already started up the stairs.

Shurik was awake. He smiled weakly and tried to sit up.

"Shurik, this is Dr. Stern. He would like to help you. He's a wonderful doctor," I said. I helped him take his coat off.

"Zdrastvooyte," Shurik said politely, extending his thin little hand in a grown-up manner.

"Zdrastvooi!" answered Dr. Stern, shaking Shurik's hand. "How are you feeling?"

"Not so good. I have pains all over."

"Well, we'll see what is wrong." Dr. Stern took a collapsible, old-fashioned listening tube from his pocket, adjusted it and pressed it to Shurik's chest. The tube was cold, and I could see Shurik's skin pucker in hundreds of tiny goose-pimples.

The doctor examined Shurik thoroughly, completely absorbed in what he was doing, paying no attention to my inquisitive glances.

When he was through, he turned to me with a broad smile.

"Get us some hot tea, woman!" he commanded, sounding like a rough peasant. Unexpectedly Shurik giggled.

"You said it just like grandpa used to say it to my grandma!" he said, still giggling.

"I am a grandpa!" declared Dr. Stern. "I have hundreds of grandchildren. All the children in the world are my grandchildren!"

"I don't believe you!" Shurik challenged.

I was amazed. My Shurik was showing signs of life again!

"Doctor, you still didn't tell me what's wrong with him," I reminded my chief.

"Nothing's wrong. He just has a very nasty bronchitis.

His lungs are clear. With good care, in a day or two he'll be as good as new. Let him stay in bed and feed him all the goodies that we brought with us. Here's some aspirin for him. Give him two tablets every four hours, and his fever will be gone by tomorrow. He is a strong, wiry lad; he won't stay sick much longer. Will you, Shurik?"

"No, doctor. I won't." Then a sudden fear flashed across his emaciated face. "But when I get better, you won't send me away, will you?" Shurik clutched the blanket with both hands, as if seeking protection against the fate which might dispatch him to the impersonal world of some unknown orphanage.

"No, darling, no! We won't send you away. I promise!" I cried and instantly wondered how I could keep such a promise.

Dr. Stern frowned. I knew that he disapproved of my action, but he said nothing. Shurik looked with uneasiness at Dr. Stern, but the chief pretended not to notice it.

"I'll make some tea," I said gaily, trying to ease the heavy uncertainty which hung in the air like a sticky fog.

"Doctor?" Shurik said timidly.

"Yes?"

"Can you promise, too, that you won't send me away?"

Dr. Stern shifted uneasily in the chair. He was on the spot, and he knew it.

"What do you mean?" he asked, stalling for time.

"I mean, will you send me to an orphanage when I get better? You're her commander, so if you order that I be sent away, she'll have to obey, even though she promised to keep me."

"I'll tell you the truth, Shurik," Dr. Stern said seriously. "According to our law we must send you to an orphanage."

Shurik's face, which only moments ago was bright with expectation, became sorrowful again. He closed his eyes wearily and once again became a listless, sick child.

"Then I don't want to get well," he whispered.

"What kind of talk is that?" Dr. Stern exploded with indignation. "You came to a wrong conclusion. You didn't let me finish. I said 'according to our law' and it's true. But there are always exceptions. Are you listening to me, boy? Open your eyes!"

Obediently Shurik opened his huge blue eyes, which seemed to be sunk in their sockets, and looked directly at Dr. Stern.

"There are always exceptions," repeated Dr. Stern. "Furthermore, I believe that in this case we have a right to claim a genuine exception. You're not an orphan. You still have your father, and as far as we know, your mother might still be alive. So you're not an orphan. Why do you keep talking such nonsense? Who's insisting on sending you away?" In spite of his own better judgment, Dr. Stern found himself—just like I—promising to keep Shurik out of an orphanage.

"Then you do promise that you won't send me away?" insisted my charge.

"I promise."

Shurik smiled happily. Then he pulled himself to a sitting position and reached for a salami sandwich.

Far Out
the Long Canal

MEINDERT DeJONG

*In the Dutch village of Wierum, everyone
can skate. Everyone, that is, except
nine-year-old Moonta. He can't because
he was sick the last time there was any
ice on the canal, and that was four winters
ago. So only the village babies—and
Moonta—are learning to skate. And
Moonta feels it keenly, so keenly he
cannot even eat when the canal freezes
and his champion-skating family agrees
he can learn.*

Canal Holiday

Somehow Moonta's nervous fingers, fumbling with every button, at last got him dressed. It was taking five times too long. After that he was as clumsy as a baby with its first shoestring. He fumbled and fumbled, then just tied both shoestrings with knots. Mother was making the beds. She had climbed on a chair, and was tucking in the corners of the one high bed with a square measuring stick. She happened to glance down, saw Moonta tying his shoestrings in knots. She made him tie them properly. "If they dangle," she said, "a skate cutting through a loose shoestring can give you a nasty fall. It could send you right over your little chair, and while that would be wonderful acrobatics, it's not good skating."

Moonta grumped, and did as he was told.

"My, I'm glad you didn't get pneumonia," Mother said. "You're not hiding it? You're really not sick? Maybe you're not feeling anything because you're so excited at going skating."

"I'm fine," Moonta said.

"Well, then—your porridge is standing ready on the kitchen table, and two good stiff hunks of black bread with cheese. That should fortify you for at least part of the morning. Oh, I'm glad you're feeling fine. You're not hiding anything?"

Moonta straightened from his shoe-tying job, made an impatient motion with his head, and rushed to the kitchen.

As he hitched his chair to the table, the steam from the hot bowl of porridge curled up around his nose. He gagged. He couldn't eat—he was all jelly inside; he was quivering. He retched at the thick, sweet smell of the porridge, and looked about to see if there was any place he could dump it where Mother wouldn't find it. There wasn't any place. Instead he jumped up and ran to the living room to get his skates. He laid the skates on the table; maybe it would help him to eat if he kept his eyes on the skates. It didn't help. He gagged from the smell of the curly steam. He jumped up again, found a piece of newspaper, and frumpled it around the thick slices of bread and cheese, and ran to his jacket and shoved them in the pocket.

Now at least he wouldn't have to eat those. It was even good. If he got the sick gape-hunger on the ice, he'd have something to cure it.

Moonta got back to his chair just in time. Mother came into the kitchen. She shoved his chair farther under the table. Now his whole face was over the sickening porridge. He tried hard to keep from retching. "I put extra sugar in it—that makes for pep, strength, and energy,"

Mother said cheerily. "Now I'll get dressed for skating, and then we'll go out to the canal. Except for eating, not a lick more of housework all day. It's to be a complete holiday on the canal. So spoon up that porridge."

He turned unwillingly back to the porridge, but he felt so sick he lied right out to Mother—outrageously. "I ate the bread," he said, "but, Mother, I can't eat any porridge. I can't."

"It's the excitement," Mother said. "We'll leave it for noon—you watch yourself wolf it then. Bundle up well. There's nothing worse than standing around on ice all sweated up."

"I'm not going to stand; I'm going to skate," he said smartly.

Fortunately Mother was too busy getting herself ready to notice he was being smart. But after he was in his jacket and muffler and stocking cap, she really examined him. She pulled and tugged, and straightened and ordered things. Then she grabbed her skates.

Moonta grabbed his skates and dashed ahead of her. "Race you down the hall," he yelled.

"I'm a dignified old lady," Mother joked. "I don't race down halls, but I'll race you on the ice."

"Next year," he said. "Next year I'll beat the stuffings right out of you."

"What an expression to use to a dignified old lady,"

Mother said, coming on slowly, walking very straight—just to tease him.

Moonta had the outer door open and held it for Mother. "Now that's proper treatment," Mother said. But she stopped doubtfully in the doorway. "Hey, wind," she said. "Where's it coming from, over land or over sea? That's important for continuing ice. If the wind shifts . . ."

Moonta looked anxiously across the street. Ah, Lees was there, leaning over her half door. "Lees, what about the wind?" he yelled. "Is it shifting? Will the ice last?"

"It may, or it may not," Lees said, looking up at the sky. "I've got a lot of sewing to do, but I'm thinking of sneaking in a little skating tomorrow—outside the village, of course. I could do that better than sew on Sunday—my rattly old sewing machine gives me away."

Everything settled in Moonta, everything seemed better now. If Lees figured on skating tomorrow, well, then, there'd be ice tomorrow. Mother must have figured the same way, for she closed the door and set the broom upside down against it to show there was nobody home. Then she thought of it. "Oh, we forgot your little red chair," she said. "It's up in the attic."

Moonta shoved his skates into Mother's hands, knocked the broom down, yanked both door halves open, and tore back into the house.

"It's too cold to stand still," Mother called after him. "I'll walk on, and you can catch up with me—you've got eager, young legs."

Up in the attic Moonta didn't look about, but tore into the mass of things piled tier on tier against the end wall. The high pile was an assortment of everything. Everything except a red chair. Moonta wildly tugged at things, hoping that behind some box or bunched bedding he'd catch a glimpse of something red. Then an old, moth-eaten feather bed sagged away from the wall, folded in the middle as if it had a terrible stomach ache, sagged to the floor. There was the little red chair! It had been propped under the soft feather bed to hold it against the wall. Moonta waded over the billowy bed— it was almost like wading in water—and grabbed the chair.

He gave the whole untidy, tumbled mess one glance and a hopeless shrug of his shoulder, and lunged down the stairway with his chair. At the foot of the stairs he looked back and carefully closed the stairway door.

Outside he didn't bother about setting the broom upside down against the closed door. People would know they weren't home—nobody was home this day, everybody was on the canal. You could hear them screaming and yelling and shrilling. Nobody was home—he was the only one, all because of the miserable chair.

Moonta raced down the street. It had taken him so long to find the chair, he didn't catch up with Mother until he got to the Main Street end of the canal.

"Well, that took you long," Mother said.

"It was way back under everything," Moonta panted.

"Sure, and I suppose you let it all lie as it fell—for me to pick up later."

Moonta bleakly nodded. He had no words. He stood astounded and open-mouthed. He felt dismayed and let down. Everybody, the whole village—young and old—everybody was on the ice. The canal was black with squirming, squiggling, racing people. It looked mad. People skated everywhere in every direction, and yelled and shouted and laughed and sang. It was unbelievable that they didn't crash and tumble all over each other and land in heaps. Long lines of twenty to thirty people behind each other, hands clasped, came bearing down on other long snaking lines. Miraculously they always missed each other, swept around each other, whiplashed in great snaking curves around still other lines, then swung and swayed in an excitement of bodies and noise and dark clothes on white ice.

In the midst of all the long dangerous-looking lines, people singly or in pairs calmly went skating on their own way, to some point that only they knew. All kinds of little kids were scooting and scratching and scrambling around. People shot up the canal, down the canal, across the canal, and on long crisscrossing slants and even in and out among the canal boats frozen into the ice. The end of the canal was so crowded there did not seem room for one more skater. Certainly there was no room for a chair.

"Look at it, look at it," Mother said. "They're starved for skating, they're giddy with it. Everybody's been yelling up at me while I stood here. They don't care what they say; they don't even know. Everything is fun."

Moonta said nothing. He stared in dismay.

"I must say, I've been standing here dithering myself," Mother said. "I'm all quirky and little jiggles keep running up my legs to get on the ice. I thought you'd never come."

With Mother talking about her jiggly feet, Moonta noticed she had already tied her skates on. Now she let herself down the bank. She reached up her arms, "First hand me your chair, then hand me you."

Moonta held back. "I'm not going down there. Mother, there's nobody skating with chairs, just two little kids that still can't do anything but skate on their ankles. They're not half as big as I am." He eyed all the darkness of the people, the whirl and the weaving and the wild, noisy busyness. He looked at the row of seven canal boats. "Mother," he asked in a small voice, "couldn't we start

beyond the canal boats, there aren't nearly so many people there? There isn't room here."

Mother frowned. "Nonsense," she said firmly. "It may
look that way from the top of the bank, but you'll see
when you get down here with me that there's plenty of
room. You'll see—people will make way; you won't run
into them or they into you."

At that moment a line of thirty or forty boys—from
the fifth and sixth grades in school—came driving straight
toward Mother. The end of the fierce skating line whipped
in such a tight sweep around Mother that her skirts rippled and billowed out. The boys dug in their sharp skate
heels and scraped to a halt in a fine high spray of ice dust
and snow. Even before the whole line had stopped they
were all yelling: "Mrs. Riemersma, where's Riemer?
Where's your husband? We want him to lead our line."

"He's gone on the Eleven-Towns Tour," Mother said.

"Oh, then will you lead us? Please?" They crowded
around Mother. "Please, we're having a race with the
men, and we want to race the young fellows too. And
maybe with you in the lead we'll win. We've got the
master with us—he's the tail end, but he's holding us
back. He's a drag and an anchor, so we need you to
lead."

Moonta looked on with alarmed eyes. There behind the
whole tight group of boys was the headmaster. He stood,

breathing too hard to say anything. He took off his woolen cap, and steam actually come up from under it. Moonta was astounded to hear the boys talk that way about the headmaster where he could hear every word they said. Anything seemed to go on the ice.

"Yes, Mrs. Riemersma," the headmaster panted. "You lead them, won't you? They ought to win at least once from the old men. With me all they can beat is some women, and they've been trying so hard."

Then the headmaster noticed Moonta up on the bank with the red chair. "Hey, Moonta," he said. "Going to teach your mother skating? I see you brought a chair."

Everybody laughed. Moonta colored and felt small and silly. Mother looked at him. At last he managed to stammer, "Oh, no, Master, I'm teaching the little red chair."

"Don't 'Master' me today, Moonta," the headmaster ordered. "Today I'm one of the boys—except that they say I'm nothing but an old rusty anchor. . . . What do you say—if you loan them your mother, and I stop being their anchor—that you and I go skate together with the chair? Is that a fair deal? Fellows, listen," he yelled to the babbling, crowding big graders around Mother. "Listen a minute, will you? Moonta's giving you the loan of his mother, to beat the old men and maybe even the young fellows in a good race. Moonta's still got to learn to skate, because he was sick the last winter we had ice.

Hey, that seems long ago—I was younger then; nobody was calling me a drag anchor then."

They yelled back jokes at the headmaster, they yelled up at Moonta all kinds of excited, bright, crazy things. The headmaster lifted Moonta down, chair and all. Nobody laughed at him or poked fun; they all thought it so wonderful that they could have Mother as the leader of their line.

Then Mother was saying to them, "Lay on, lay on." They all stopped their kidding and quickly formed a line by putting clasped hands behind their backs for the one behind to grasp.

"It's all right, isn't it, Moonta?" Mother called over her shoulder as the line started slowly away. Her cheeks were red with excitement. "You'll be in good hands."

"Sit down on that chair and I'll tie your skates, and then I'll watch you skate to see if they need any adjustment to one side or the other," the headmaster ordered.

To Moonta's amazement, when the headmaster had finished, he wanted to try the little chair. He had to bend over nearly double, he stuck out behind most undignified, but he went skating away with the little red chair straight across the canal, right in among the thickest crowd. He made a great loop, then came swooping back where Moonta stood plastered up against the canal bank.

As he neared Moonta the headmaster sent the chair flying and twisting over the ice. "Try it," he yelled.

"Moonta, this is it! What I wouldn't have given for a little chair like this when I had to learn to skate. But in the part of the country where I was born, I guess no-body had the brains to think of such a simple way to learn. . . . Try it, you've got to try it."

Moonta caught the little chair on the fly, grabbed a tight hold on the back, and like that he was skating. He was skating, he was skating! He went in a big loop just like the headmaster had done, and then he came back straight at the master. "Oh, it's so easy, Master; it's just like that," he yelled.

"Isn't it?" the headmaster said. "But don't you 'Master' me today, I said, not on the ice." He skated beside Moonta; they went straight down the canal. It was miraculous, for while from the high bank it looked to be impossible to find even a square yard of room for himself and the chair, now somehow people that were in the way weren't there when he and the chair got there.

When once in a while Moonta got in people's way, they just swirled dizzily around him, or braked by digging their sharp skate heels into the ice.

Nobody poked fun at the chair, nobody even thought of poking fun. Of course that might have been because the headmaster was skating with him. Still it didn't seem so. People that on the streets took off their caps to the headmaster, here on the ice just yelled anything out at him as he skated past. And the headmaster yelled back anything that came into his head. It seemed anything went on the ice.

Now Moonta excitedly twisted his head back to see how far they had come. Then when he turned back, an old man was in the chair's way. He did not get out of the way as fast as Moonta had expected; he was stiff and slow. The headmaster grabbed the chair, swirled Moonta and chair around in a tight circle—if he hadn't, Moonta would have knocked the old man down. Instead Moonta and chair and headmaster went down in a heap and a tangle, but not the old man. He hadn't noticed anything. Now he stopped in surprise and looked down on the fallen headmaster.

"Master," he said, "you down there? But that's what comes of bringing furniture on the ice."

Moonta held his breath, but the headmaster just laughed as he scrambled to his feet and didn't even blame Moonta. In a way he blamed the old man. "Siebren," he said, "I can see you didn't learn with a chair. In fact, I know, because like me, you're from another part of the country. But I can tell you if you had learned with a chair you could have got out of our way on time. Why, man, Monday I'll be here skating on behind the lectern from my schoolroom."

Old man Siebren looked up at the sky. He wet his

thumb and held it up. "That lectern might not be a bad idea by Monday," he said. "But bring a couple of oars, too; you'll be sitting in it and using it as a boat. Mark my word, the wind's shifting to the wrong corner. By Monday this canal will be water again."

The headmaster just grinned. "I can't stand weather prophets," he said. "Especially old ones that can't get out of our way." He took hold of Siebren. "Come on, old man, let's you and me strike out for the bend of the canal beyond the village and get out from underfoot. And I'll bet you in another hour or so this Moonta will come racing past us—without a chair."

It was wonderful now. Oh, it was exciting, skating on alone. Moonta had only to remember not to keep looking at the wonder of his flying feet, and of his skates stroking across the ice. It *was* a flying feeling.

Just ahead of him a long line of young women—why, it was Af in the lead—went down in a terrible heap right beside the headmaster and old Siebren. One of them reached out and clawed herself upright by pulling herself up by the headmaster. He lost his balance and went down among the heap of women. He scrambled to his feet, stood over them, and hooted: "What a clumsy bunch of old women."

"Old women!" the young women screeched as they scrambled up. "Why, we're hardly out of your musty old school. . . . Grab him, girls," Af was shrieking. "Grab him, put him in the middle of our line. We'll teach him, we'll make him skate with us 'old women.' "

The headmaster had no chance at all. The line reformed, he was put in the middle. They swooped away with him in their midst. Everybody that saw it hooted and yelped and cat-called.

Old man Siebren had stayed on his feet. He still stood there looking bewildered and shaking his head. Moonta skated up to him with the red chair. Boldly he asked the old man, "Will you please watch my chair just a moment?"

Before slow old Siebren could think what to say, Moonta skated away without the chair. For thirty, forty, fifty strokes it went fine, then Moonta smashed hard to the ice. He had to lie still for a long moment in surprise and shock. Then, looking alongside himself, he saw one of his shoestrings was dangling. It had caught under his skate. It was nearly cut in two. Moonta angrily yanked the cut piece away, at the same time glad and relieved it was the shoestring that had made him fall. He scrambled to his feet, hoping Siebren hadn't seen him. Then he noticed Siebren wasn't where he had left him. He had skated away. Old as he was, now he was trying the chair.

Moonta raced after him, but when he caught up, the old man didn't give up the chair. Moonta had to skate beside Siebren the way the headmaster had skated beside him. It was a proud wonder. Old Siebren kept saying,

"If I could only bend better, boy. This is the thing, this is the thing. Guess I'll have to get me a lectern, like the master—or a sawhorse, or something."

Just then Mother and her whole line of boys came bearing down on them in a fury of skating. As she swept by, Mother called out, "Having fun, Moonta? Having fun?"

"Teaching Siebren, now," Moonta yelled back.

The long line ripped by. It actually felt as if the ice yielded and bent, almost rippled a little from their weight. In a flash Mother was gone. But the last boy in the line, the biggest sixth grader, turned his head. He yelled out at Moonta as he snaked and whipped along, "We beat the men, we're going out to find the young fellows now. We'll beat them for you, Moonta. They're the ones that made you a 'pickerel.' "

"Beat the living daylights out of them," Moonta yelled back. "Beat them hollow. Chase them under the bridge into the water hole. Drown them." He didn't mean it at all; it was just that everything was so exciting, it was something exciting to yell. It made him seem a part of them. He stood and watched them out of sight—enviously. But old Siebren had skated on with the chair; he had to take out after Siebren again. He scratched and he scrabbled.

This time the old man gave up the chair. It felt good

to lean on it again. Now with his chair Moonta dared to skate faster and faster. He practiced quick shifts and darts, loops and circles. Then he even dared to take it and weave in and out among the thickest crowd at the Main Street end of the canal.

When he looked up, there was Aunt Cora standing on the high bank. She was watching everything so hard she didn't see him. He skated toward her until he stood right below her. "Aunt Cora," he yelled, "Aunt Cora, oh, this is fun. I'm learning to skate, and I can skate without my chair. Watch my chair, will you? I'll show you." He shoved the chair against the bank and skated away into the thick of the crowd. He felt himself skating so well he couldn't resist—anxious to see that Aunt Cora was watching him—throwing a look up over his shoulder. Like that he smashed to the ice. He'd been looking back, there wasn't time to throw up his hands. He hit the ice flat with his face.

He slowly lifted his head, looked alongside himself, but this time he had not cut a shoestring. His laces were tied. He lay shamed, angry, and mortified. Right before Aunt Cora he'd smashed down like a fool.

"Moonta, Moonta," Aunt Cora cried. "Are you hurt?"

He yelled, "NO." He refused to look up at her. Something warm crawled through the mitten on the hand with which he was holding himself up from the ice. It was

117

blood. He was bleeding. He mashed his mittened hand to his nose. The blood guttered, his whole mitten went red.

Somebody swooped over him, scooped him up, lifted him to his feet. It was Mother. "Oh, Moonta," she said, "I was watching you; you were doing so well behind your chair, then you had to go and show off. Look at you!" She was angry because she was worried. She skated away with him, holding him, half lifting him. She hoisted him up to Aunt Cora. She tossed his chair up after him. Now Aunt Cora held him and started stooping over him in front of all the people on the ice.

Aunt Cora was worried too. "Ice is supposed to stop a nose bleed, not give you one," she joked nervously. She ripped the white scarf off her head, bundled it, and stuffed it under his nose. In no time the white scarf was a red mess.

Moonta was angry, and if the scarf hadn't been practically rammed into his mouth he would have yelled out at Aunt Cora, "You should talk—Father said you were always smashing yourself bloody-nosed." He didn't say it. When he opened his mouth blood ran into it from under the scarf.

He saw all the people standing looking up at him. Mother was crouched, taking her skates off. The next moment the canal swam before Moonta's eyes. The whole canal blackened and seemed full of queer, mixed-up, blotchy, ballooning figures.

"I'm sick," he gasped from under the scarf to Aunt Cora. "I feel queer. I'm cold, but I'm sweating, and my knees are shaking."

"Don't talk," Aunt Cora ordered. "Swallowing blood will only make you sicker."

"Mother, I'm sick," Moonta said miserably as he saw his mother come scrambling up the bank.

But Aunt Cora laughed now. "Don't be scared, Moonta, you're not bleeding to death. What you've got is gape-hunger. Bet you couldn't eat any breakfast this morning, and the cold and hard work on skates . . ."

"Thank goodness, if that's what it is," Mother said. Then she plumped herself down on Moonta's little chair. "Why, I'm sick myself. I've got the ice-hunger too. I must confess—like any school girl—I couldn't eat breakfast either."

Then Moonta remembered. "I've got the bread with cheese in my jacket pocket."

Mother reached over into Moonta's pocket and dug out the newspaper-wrapped bread. Aunt Cora took the scarf away and studied Moonta's smeared face. "It's stopped," she said. "You're going to live. That is, if you two skate-crazy people will let me run to my house and quick fix you a lunch." She stooped to take off Moonta's skates.

Mother stuffed half a slice of black bread into her mouth; she reached up and stuffed the other half into

Moonta's mouth. "Why, what time is it?" she demanded, over her mouthful.

"Almost noon," Aunt Cora said.

Mother shook her head unbelievingly. "My, good time goes fast. Sure, run ahead. We two starved skeletons will come rattling on after we eat this."

Almost together Moonta and Mother swallowed their huge mouthfuls of bread and cheese. Almost together they said "Ah."

"Doesn't that clear up the eyes and brighten things?" Mother asked, even as she stuffed her mouth full again.

"I can see straight again," Moonta exclaimed. "Mother, I thought I was dying."

"Well, now that you haven't," Mother said, getting up and picking up the little red chair, "what say you and I stagger home toward more food?"

It was amazing how flat-footed and stiff he walked, Moonta thought. His ankles were as stiff as wood. Without skates under his feet he put his feet down so flat and hard, he felt like an old, plodding plow horse. Mother walked exactly the same way. Why, they walked like two tired old stiff people—with rheumatism in both legs.

Mother laughed as they looked down on themselves. "Now you know how it feels to be an earthling again, after feeling almost like a flying eagle. Isn't it awful? You almost feel as if you were a seal trying to get ahead on your flippers."

Oh, that was funny what Mother had said. "Mother," Moonta asked, "how do I skate?"

"You've got good skating feet—good ankles, and a good stroke. You're going to be a good skater."

Moonta glowed. "Then can we leave the chair home after lunch?"

Mother shook her head. "No, you're too reckless. You want to go at it too fast. Still skate with the chair this afternoon. Don't worry, I'll watch, and the moment I think you're ready, I'll toss the chair up on one of the canal boats, and you can practice without it."

"Then are we going to the New Church's Pipe?"

"We'll see, we'll see—one thing at a time. If you could only get that through your head, you wouldn't be a bloody-nosed mess now. You're trying to do too much too fast."

"But you said we were going to the Pipe," Moonta yammered. "And now just because I've got a bloody nose, you're all scared. . . . Would we have gone if I hadn't got a bloody nose?"

"It didn't help," Mother said shortly.

It seemed so outrageous that just a bloody nose might keep him from getting to the New Church's Pipe, Moonta thought up a barefaced lie. "I fell because I had a loose shoelace, and my skate cut through it," he said angrily. "I can skate, you saw me when old Siebren had my chair."

"Moonta!" Mother said, shocked. "You lie! Just because I was skating with those boys; you may not have known it, but I was keeping an eye on you all the time. I saw you cut through your shoelace and throw the piece away where somebody else could trip on it and crash down. You lied this morning about eating the bread, too. And just because you're dead set to get to that Pipe is not any excuse for lying like that. You watch it, lad; a lying mouth, more than a bloody nose, is exactly what may stop me from going with you to that New Church's Pipe."

When Mother said "lad," and when she talked as if she were reading it from the Bible, Moonta knew it was time to be quiet. Still, the next moment it seemed he had to start again, even though he changed the subject a little. "If we don't get to go to the Pipe, then this afternoon can I get in one of those long lines behind you?"

Mother laughed at him. "Behind me, or would you rather be the lead after a couple of hours of beginning to learn to skate?"

"No, the last one," Moonta said promptly. "I'd like to be the tail-ender. He really gets whipped around. When he has to let go just from sheer speed at the end of a sweep, he flies like a bullet."

"Exactly," Mother said. "That's it exactly. There you go again always wanting what is the most dangerous and reckless."

"Oh, all right," he grouched, "then I won't. I'll just get in the middle of your line." They were at Aunt Cora's house. Moonta hobbled ahead to open the door for Mother—to make things right after his grouching. "Mother . . ." he began.

As she stepped into the hall Mother whirled on him. "Get in the middle," she said indignantly. "You'll get right behind that chair, and you'll stay there as long as I say so. And no more begging me for anything. Isn't there ever going to be an end? Moonta, why must you be such a whining baby with me, and such a roughneck outside?"

"I don't know," he said slowly. "I guess maybe it's because I've got to do everything right now while there's ice. Don't you think I want to be a champion too?"

"Well," Mother said. "I don't know . . . I've been wondering if tomorrow in church I shouldn't pray for a big thaw."

"No, Mother," Moonta said, horrified. "That's the whole trouble—if a thaw comes too soon. Mother, won't you, please, pray the other way?"

Mother just looked at him. It was time to be still—way past time.

February Dragon

COLIN THIELE

Country living can be full of excitement in the Australian summer; and children like Resin, Turps and Columbine Pine savor its fun while they dread the quick danger that can flare across sun-dried acres.

ld Barnacle's store stood at the side of the dusty road that ran from Summertown to Upper Gumbowie. A sprawling, ramshackle, delicious old store it was, dim and untidy inside, and crowded with everything that was ever made. The children loved it. As soon as they pushed open the warped screen door and pressed their bare feet on the worn grain and knotty little knolls of the wooden floorboards, they were walking in a different world. It was a world that smelled of onions and harness leather; camphor balls, pepper, and sour cucumbers. A world littered and cluttered with magic: rabbit traps and jams, axes, saws, sprockets, and eggs; slabs of bacon, cans of molasses and paint, pens, marshmallows, and rope; long straight sausages and heavy-heeled working boots; open bags of sugar with half-swallowed scoops in their throats; butter, bolts, mixed biscuits, and salt; cans of herring and tomato sauce; jars of honey and bottles of brightly colored cordials and essences; sweets, saucepans, vinegar, currants, clocks, shirts, fleecy-lined pajamas, carbolic acid, cod-liver oil; and all the wonderful tastes, smells, surprises, and dreams that lay unknown in hidden cupboards and on dark mysterious shelves.

In the two little dim display windows, the blowflies

buzzed monotonously up and down against the glass, or lay silently on their backs with their legs in the air. At one end of the counter stood a row of pigeonholes, a pair of scales, an inkstand, and a mess of papers—blotters, booklets, stamp pads, and old envelopes. This was the Post Office, and somewhere in the midst of all this, at the counter, behind the groceries, among the hardware, out through the back door, on the veranda, or halfway up the shelves, you would always find Old Barnacle. He never seemed to leave the place. He was as permanent as the daddy-long-legs spiders, and the strange, sweet-sour smells that lived in the store forever. He was gruff and grumpy, crusty and cranky, shrewd and kind, all at once, and he knew every boy and girl in the district better than their own fathers did. . . .

Pets

Not far from Old Barnacle's store Resin, Turps, and Columbine lived in a wide, shady house at the end of the scrub. The gum trees and wattles, blackbutts, she-oaks, and native pines came jostling down the slope almost to the back door. Then, just as it looked as though they were going to trample over the farmyard and the sheds and

Mrs. Pine's vegetable garden, they sidestepped, and veered off along the edges of the cleared land, sweeping and tossing their leaves and branches in the spring wind. People called the uncleared land "The Big Scrub." It stretched far off toward the South Australian border, except where it was broken up by farms or roads or telephone lines. Everyone called the house "Bottlebrush Barn," which was the name Dad gave to the shack he had built there after the war, when he first started clearing the land.

A little later, when he married, he had built the shady house, with the great vines climbing up the verandas, but it was still called Bottlebrush Barn. Sometimes their mother scolded about the name. "Harry Pine," she'd say, "I wish you would stop calling the place a barn. What must people think?" But Dad laughed. "It's a good name," he'd say, "and everybody knows it, so let it stay." And it stayed.

The nearest school was fifteen miles away in Upper Gumbowie, and the narrow road from the Barn twisted and ducked among the trees, swept down into creek beds, panted over ridges, shot along straight fences past farms and clearings, and finally looped happily into the town. In the mornings the school bus rattled and darted, and stopped and started, for fifteen miles, on its way southward along the road, and in the afternoons it rattled and darted, and stopped and started, fifteen miles back again.

It always spent the night at George Dobson's farmhouse, about a mile up the road from Bottlebrush Barn, because that was where Miss Strarvy lived. He was the teacher who drove the bus. His real name was Mr. Harvey, but people never seemed to have time to pause between the "Mr." and the "Harvey" when they were speaking, so they made "Miss Strarvy" out of it.

At twenty to eight every morning the bus started with a terrifying snort, and wobbled off slowly out of a cloud of smoke, rinsed with blue in the early sunlight. Mr. and Mrs. Dobson's two children, Don and Debby, sat with their knees up on the backseat. Miss Strarvy pumped the accelerator and the choke, grazed the big strainer post by the farmyard gate, and careered down the road, straightening his coat collar with his left hand as he drove along, and whistling "Waltzing Matilda" so loudly that his lips looked like the underside of a mushroom. At Bottlebrush Barn he stopped with a lurch, calling out "Good morning, everyone" in a cheerful voice, long before Resin, Turps, and Columbine could get on the bus. "Morning, sir," they'd say in a chorus, and walk with big strides down the center of the bus to join the other two at the back.

Resin, whose real name was Melton, was nearly twelve —big and tawny-haired, he liked wearing long pants and an old Army slouch hat that Dad had brought back from the war. Dad was proud of Resin. "Be running the farm in a year or two," he'd say. "Reckon I can retire then." Turps, who had been christened Crystal, was ten—bright-eyed and spindle-shanked. And little Colin, whom everyone called Columbine instead of Colin Pine, was only six. Resin had started junior-high work; Turps, Don, and Debby were all in the same elementary grade; and little Columbine was still in kindergarten.

And so Miss Strarvy's bus whooped happily through the trees or ground the teeth of its gears up the ridges, collecting more and more children from the gates and corners and tracks and milk shelters until the seats were crowded. Brenda Wilson was there, and Bridget and Bill O'Brien, and the Hammond children, and Burp Heaslip, and a dozen more. Burp's name was really "Bert," but once when Columbine was just a toddler and couldn't talk properly, he'd called him "Burp" and everyone had laughed so much that the name had stuck. Luckily Burp didn't mind at all. He had a freckled face as round as a tin plate with rust spots all over it, and he always laughed or grinned about nothing at all.

"Here we are," Miss Strarvy would say as the bus rollicked up the road to the Upper Gumbowie School. "Five minutes before bell time." And everyone would shoot out onto the footpath like gravel from a dump truck.

All through the day they worked side by side with the

children from Upper Gumbowie, just as if they all lived together in the town. But at four o'clock the bus travelers split up again and rushed outside to wait for Miss Strarvy, and by five o'clock they were being unloaded at the end of the run, dropped off onto the dusty road like sacks with legs. Soon only the Pines and the Dobsons were left. Then Resin, Turps, and Columbine clattered off, and Don and Debby were alone for the last mile to their home, where the bus and Miss Strarvy rested again until the next morning.

Bottlebrush Barn was a wonderful place for pets. To begin with, there was a huge black mountain of a mongrel tomcat, two feet long and one foot high, called "Puss'll-do." He had somehow been left with this queer name years before, when no one could suggest what the new black kitten should be called. Eventually they had turned to Mr. Pine.

"Dad, you give him a name. No matter what you call him, we'll agree with you."

"Oh, Puss'll do," Dad had said casually, and so Puss'll-do it was, and Puss'll-do it had remained.

As well as the big black tomcat there were three dogs on the farm, five calves, two pet lambs, thirteen piglets, half a dozen goats, a pair of black rabbits, four other cats, two ferrets, and a cockatoo. Admittedly the calves were not really house pets, but Resin and Turps had to help feed them, and so they christened each one and spoke of it as part of the farmyard.

In addition to the dozens of usual pets—the ones Resin called "regulars"—there were two outsiders. One was Jacky, the kookaburra, who turned up once or twice a week at daybreak and flew straight at Mrs. Pine's bedroom window. It was a signal to let everyone in the house know that he was hungry and that it was time to get up. He struck the glass with such a crash, it made the frame creak and brought Mr. Pine leaping out of bed like a thunderclap.

"All right, all right," he'd yell. "Blast it all, there's no need to smash the window!" And he'd quickly get some juicy lumps of meat from the refrigerator and throw them out by the kitchen door. For a while nothing would happen. The trees would sigh, and the wind nudge lightly about the house. Then there would be a shadowy rush of brown wings in the dim light as Jacky came swooping in to snatch up the morsels. A moment later he would be gone again in a blur, and there would suddenly be a new stump of wood, sitting quite motionless, high up on the branch of a nearby tree. As the daylight grew, Jacky would think things over for a while until the idea of Mr. Pine leaping out of bed in his pajamas tickled his fancy so much that he would fling back his head and laugh till the hillside rang, and the feathers under his open beak shook as if he were gargling his throat with the light from the rising sun. At last, when he had finished his joke, he flew away silently, and nobody saw him again for three or four days.

The other outsider was Gus. He came and went even more secretly than Jacky. But five or six times a year somebody was sure to stumble on him with a start and a thrill of surprise, and race up to the house, yelling, "Hey, Gus is back, I just saw him—he's as big as a croc!" Mrs. Pine wasn't quite so keen about Gus as the others were. For Gus was a goanna, a big bull bush goanna, five feet long. He had a body like an alligator's, a long tapering tail, a slim neck with a shovel head, and four strong legs. In the summer they would sometimes see him drinking at the cattle trough, or lying in the damp shade of a cucumber patch by the dam, and now and again someone would get a surprise to find him basking in the spring sunshine behind the haystack.

When this happened to the children, they would always jump. "Ooh, gosh!" Then, a second later, "Ah-h, it's only Gus. Hullo, Gus." Gus would raise himself slowly on all four feet until he seemed to be balancing on his claws like a dancer, his head darting gently and his eyes flashing. "It's all right, Gus. No need to be frightened." That was a joke really, because Resin and Turps, and especially young Columbine, were just as uncertain and suspicious about Gus, with his strong teeth and claws, as Gus seemed to be about them.

Then a dog would bark, or a horse stamp nearby, and Gus would be off like a rocket in a flurry of straw and whirling sticks, sweeping up toward The Big Scrub as swiftly as a long thick shadow.

"Sneaky reptile," their mother said. "I wouldn't trust that fellow any more than a fox or a ferret."

"Oh, Mum! Gus wouldn't do a thing. Honest."

Their mother mimicked them nastily.

"Oh, no, Gus wouldn't do a thing, except snoop around the fowl shed, sniffing out the eggs and little chickens with that great long tongue of his."

"But, Mum, he's a pet."

"Well, then let's bring him in by the fire like a cat and stroke his ugly scaly back every night."

"He is a pet. He knows we wouldn't hurt him."

"I'll hurt him all right if I catch him stealing my eggs. I'll take the broomstick to him." Mr. Pine laughed at that. "Leave him alone, Mum," he said; "as long as he's about, we won't be bothered with snakes."

That was how Gus got the run of Bottlebrush Barn. All except for the house and the verandas. He seemed to know that if he ventured out of the vegetable garden up to the back door, Mrs. Pine would take to him with the broomstick.

The Dragon

Sometimes tourists traveling between Adelaide and Melbourne used the road past Bottlebrush Barn for their cars and trailers. It was good, they said, to get off the main highways for a change and to see Australia by the back roads and bush tracks. But most of them didn't really see Australia at all. They swept past with engines roaring, tires whirring, and radios blaring, so that they never had a chance to see the sun shining through the green fern in the creek, or to feel the soft tickle of moss on a log with the tips of their fingers, or to smell the faint scent of a wild flower as small as a spider's eye, or to hear the talk of crickets under the bark, or the itching and clicking of insects like beetles' castanets at the end of a still summer day.

And if a cat, or possum, or rabbit didn't get out of the way, cars rushed down on them, crushing them or tossing them aside in the grass, maimed and bleeding. It was worse at night than by day. The headlights came boring through the darkness, dazzling and terrifying the animals, freezing them into statues until destruction thundered down on them.

Sometimes on a fine Sunday night Resin, Turps, and

Columbine would sit with their parents on the veranda. Now and again a car would sweep past the front gate and disappear, with its taillights glaring angrily, down the road past Old Barnacle's store.

One night as they watched, a strange thing happened. A red bullet seemed to shoot out from a passing car and whizz through the air, scattering sparks like fireworks. It hit the road and leaped off in a lovely shower of red streamers into the bush, where it stopped spinning at last and lay quite still like a tiny firefly, winking and glowing for a long time until it faded and disappeared.

"Ooh, whatever was that?" Turps yelled. "Wasn't it beautiful!"

Her father looked serious.

"It may have been beautiful," he said, "but it was the most dangerous thing in Australia."

Turps looked puzzled. "Why, Dad?"

"Because of what it was."

"What was it?"

"Fire."

"Fire?"

"A cigarette butt."

Turps was astonished. "It couldn't have been. It looked like fireworks."

"It could have given us fireworks all right," her father said ominously. "Enough to supply South Australia and Victoria too. It could have set the whole countryside alight, turned the gum trees into torches, the pines into giant sparklers, and the hillsides into rivers of fire."

"Bushfires?"

"Bushfires."

"How horrible."

Mrs. Pine straightened her knitting. Then she looked up.

"People shouldn't be allowed to throw their cigarettes and matches out of passing cars. Don't they know there's a law against it?"

Mr. Pine swatted at a mosquito.

"People are careless, Muriel. They forget they're in the bush, and they just toss out their butts as though they're driving down St. Kilda Road or over Sydney Harbor Bridge." He sighed. "Ah well, I suppose it keeps all of us on our toes, especially the E.F.S."

Resin knew well enough what that meant. He had seen the men of the Emergency Fire Service training at Upper Gumbowie. The members were ordinary men: shearers and wheat growers, truck drivers, clerks, and shopkeepers from the farms and little towns, who dropped everything and rushed off in the fire trucks whenever an alarm sounded. They spread the news by telephone, wireless, and sirens, until men came pouring toward the fire from every farm and township for miles around.

"Fires start in hundreds of ways," Mr. Pine said, "but almost always from human beings, and almost always from carelessness. Campfires, broken exhaust pipes, bad spark plugs on tractors and railway trains, magnifying glasses and empty bottles, hot ashes, incinerators, welding gear, lamps, electrical faults. But most of all from silly people with cigarettes and matches." He sat silently again for a minute.

"They don't realize that a match is nothing but a chained-up dragon. If once they let him loose, he is likely to wipe out everything for a hundred miles around."

Turps put her arms high up around her knees and shuddered. She had never thought of a match as a chained-up dragon before.

Woppit

In spite of the surprises and excitement that Gus and Jacky sometimes caused, it was one of the dogs that accidentally provided the most hair-raising incident of all. He was Woppit, an inoffensive old fellow, half kangaroo dog, half kelpie, who had been working on the farm for ten or twelve years. According to Mr. Pine he should have been pensioned off long ago, but he was still much too energetic for that. Because of his kangaroo-dog blood he could still run faster over a short distance than either of the other two dogs, Snap and Blue, and he seemed to have eyes like telescopes because, once they had seen a rabbit or a hare, they locked onto it and never lost sight of it again. As he grew older, Woppit's coat got thinner and more moth-eaten every day.

"Losing his fur, that dog of yours, ain't he, Harry?" George Dobson said to Mr. Pine one day. "Looks as if the mice have been at it."

"Yes, it's getting kind of scurfy," Mr. Pine admitted. "Must be old age."

"By yiminy, 'Arry," old Emil Eckert, their German neighbor, crowed a couple of days later, "dat dog don't grow much of a crop of hair. Never have I seen anudder dog mit a worse crop dan dat."

"It's not very thick," Mr. Pine agreed.

"Tick? Is not tick at all. Is tin, very tin."

"It is thin, I guess."

"Never haff I a tinner crop in my life seen. I t'ink d' drought he is having on his back. Notting vill grow dere no more."

"Well, there's nothing I can do about it," Mr. Pine said. "I'm not going to put hair restorer on his back."

Old Emil pushed back his felt hat and laughed. "I t'ink you better put super on it, or blood-and-bone manure perhaps."

But Mr. Pine wasn't inclined to treat it as such a joke.

"A watering with the garden hose is all he's likely to get," he said, "or maybe a good wash with soap and warm water."

"Dat vill not do much good," Emil insisted. "Look at you. You is all d' time voshing your head mit soapy water, but you is getting balder every day."

Although some of the neighbors kept on laughing at poor Woppit's coat, the Pine children were worried about it. Turps, especially, began to get angry when their friends on the school-bus run joined in and started asking whether Woppit had red dust or dandruff in his hair. A week or two later a small sore appeared on Woppit's back and Turps was really alarmed.

"There's something wrong with him," she said emphatically. "He's got a disease."

Resin agreed with her. "A skin disease. Dermatitis or something."

But their father wasn't very sympathetic. "Don't be so silly. It's not a skin disease."

"Why isn't it?"

"Because he's quite happy and comfortable. You don't see him scratching himself or rubbing his back against a post, do you?"

"No."

"Well, then, it can't be hurting or itching."

"He might be very strong-willed."

"So might my aunty."

"I still think we ought to take him to a vet."

But their father reacted very strongly to that idea. "A vet? Where do you think the nearest vet is?"

"In Summertown?"

"Yes. And I'm certainly not going to drive sixty miles in the middle of the plowing just because an old crock of a dog gets a scratch on his back."

"He's not an old crock! He's Woppit!"

"He'll be better in a week or two. Probably got a nip in a fight."

The children gave up the argument then, but they were not convinced. They decided to keep a close watch on old Woppit and to act quickly if he grew worse.

The following Saturday Mrs. Pine was seized with one of her periodic fits of spring-cleaning. It was a beautiful morning, calm and sunny. Mrs. Pine threw open both the front and back doors so that the clean air could march through the house down the main corridor, and frolic in and out through the windows, chimneys, and ventilators.

"Nothing like a good spring-cleaning to blow the cobwebs away and freshen things up a bit," she said.

Resin had escaped into The Big Scrub with his father to look for likely fence-post timber, but Turps and Columbine were in the thick of it. They brushed, scrubbed, swept, and beat until their arms ached, but their mother never paused. Five or six times they staggered out to the rubbish heap with loads of unwanted junk. Packing cases, old boots and shoes, pictures and calendars, cracked dishes, almanacs, empty flagons and bottles, cans of all shapes and sizes, piles of newspapers and magazines, an old meat cooler, cardboard boxes, wrapping paper, broken knife blades, useless toys, the confusion of bric-a-brac hoarded by everyone for years—all went out onto the dump.

"Anyone would think it was a nest for lyrebirds," their mother said a little breathlessly. "It's high time we had a good clean-out." She wielded the mop and buzzed the vacuum cleaner until the carpets were as clean and soft to the touch as a cat's fur, and the linoleum was a patterned mirror. From time to time Mrs. Pine stood back to admire everything. It was clear that she was proud of the result of her work.

Twice Turps and Columbine had to go down to Old Barnacle's store for new supplies of floor wax and brass polish. And it was on the second of these trips that the great Woppit Incident took place. Old Barnacle started it.

"Nice dog you've got there," he said, leaning over the counter and almost smiling. Turps was so surprised at this sudden and unexpected show of friendliness that she looked up quickly, suspicious that the old man had joined all the other people of the district and was really ridiculing Woppit. But Barnacle was quite serious. Turps warmed to him.

"Do you think so?" she asked, smiling.

"Of course. Seen him with your father; always liked him."

"Have you?"

"Good cut of a dog. Got a bit of kangaroo dog in him."

Turps beamed. It was one of Barnacle's rare happy days. And, although he would never admit it, he secretly liked Turps.

"Must've been a great farm dog in his time, eh?"

"Oh, yes. Wonderful."

"Clever, eh?"

"Oh, very clever. Still is."

Columbine hastened to support his sister. "He's cleverer than Snap or Bluey. Dad says he's never had a cleverer dog than Woppit." They all stood in silent admiration for a while. Then Turps' face fell. "But he's getting old. And his coat's awfully . . . well, sort of scruffy-looking."

Barnacle pooh-poohed her concern. "Nothing to worry about."

Columbine looked up at him with big bug eyes. "We think his skin is getting worn out."

Barnacle laughed. "No matter. It's what's inside that counts."

"D'you reckon?"

"Sure of it. Same with people. I don't care whether they're as smooth as babies or as wrinkled as elephants, so long as they're not rotten inside."

Columbine stepped forward earnestly. "Oh, Woppit's not rotten inside!"

"Course he's not. So what are you worrying about?"

Turps patted Woppit's moldy coat. "Well, it's gone quite bald in one patch on his back—see."

Barnacle was concerned. He put on his glasses and came bustling out from behind the counter. "Where? Which patch?"

Turps held Woppit and pointed. "There."

Barnacle bent over, peering at it for a second, and then straightened up, laughing. "Huh!" he said lightly. "A bit of scurf! I can clear it in a minute."

Columbine beamed at him. "How, Mr. Barnacle?"

Barnacle frowned at the nickname, but he let it pass. He was too concerned with remedies for the dog.

"Turps'll fix it," he said.

"How will she?"

"Just a touch on the sore spot ought to do it."

Columbine was mystified and astonished. He turned to his sister, evidently picturing in her a miracle of healing. "Gee, Turps, will it? Really?" He paused, thinking, then turned to Barnacle accusingly. "But she's touched Woppit lots of times, and it hasn't made any difference at all."

Turps suddenly understood and doubled up with

laughter. "Not *me*," she shrieked. "Mr. Billings means turpentine—the real stuff, in a bottle."

Barnacle, always pleased at the mention of his real name, joined in the laughter so unexpectedly that Turps and Columbine stopped short and looked at him. Neither of them had ever heard him laugh before.

"I'll get some," he chuckled. "Only take a minute."

Woppit sniffed about the shop while the old storekeeper was outside, as if he sensed that all the enjoyment and activity had something to do with him.

"Now it won't be long, Woppit old doggie," Barnacle said, shuffling back urgently with a bottle of turpentine in his hand. "This is the best cure in the world for scurfy backsides." He shook the bottle as though it was cough mixture. "Better come out onto the veranda; we can see better there."

They lined up outside, Turps holding Woppit by the collar while Barnacle examined him. The worst spot was a bald patch on the slope of his rump above the tail.

"Now," said Barnacle, "just hold him still for a second while I dab a bit on his back." He uncorked the bottle and took a piece of rag out of his pocket. "Might give him a bit of jip for a second or two, so you better hold him pretty tight."

"What's jip, Mr. Barnacle?" Columbine asked.

Barnacle didn't answer. Perhaps he was too busy; perhaps he considered that anyone who didn't know what jip was didn't deserve being talked to. "Now," he said, "if there's any of them virus germs on poor old Woppity here, there's nothing like turps to burn 'em out. Gets rid of 'em in no time."

He upended the bottle onto the rag. Rather more turpentine than he intended flooded out, soaking the rag and spilling onto the floor.

"Now, Woppity, there's a good dog," he said encouragingly. "This'll do you a world of good." He pressed the rag onto Woppit's back, squeezing it as he did so. Turpentine from the saturated pad ran out on both sides, trickling down Woppit's rump and tail.

"There, that'll soon fix . . ." But Barnacle didn't get any further. For with a wild yelp Woppit took off, wrenching his collar free from Turps' hand and sending poor Columbine flying head over heels off the veranda.

"Whoops!" Barnacle yelled, as if the wind had been knocked out of him; "it must be giving him a bit of jip."

"Gosh!" Turps said.

"What's the matter with him?" Columbine asked, picking himself up.

They both looked at Barnacle. For the second time that day he was laughing. "Hey! Hey! Look at him go! By golly, that dog is fast."

"Is it hurting him?" Turps asked, dismayed.

"Just a bit of jip. He'll soon calm down!"

But it was quite clear that the turpentine was giving

Woppit plenty of jip. After catapulting from the veranda he raced around in a series of swooping curves, leaping high like a vaulter and swerving and twisting about in midair, trying to bite his back.

"Poor Woppit," Turps cried. "It must be stinging terribly."

"Won't be long," Barnacle said reassuringly, "and he'll be quiet as a lamb again."

But Woppit didn't get as quiet as a lamb. After rolling over and over in the dirt for a minute, he suddenly straightened up and shot off toward Heaslips' dam. They ran out and watched him going down the track, ears flattened and body arching to the rhythm of his speed. As he reached the dam, he leaped off the bank, plunging headlong into the water with a huge splash. As far as they could make out, he wriggled about furiously in the dam for a minute or two before he floundered out, rolled about in the mud and dirt again, and came rocketing back toward the main road. Turps and Columbine ran out to try to intercept him.

"Woppit! Woppit! Here, boy!" Turps called. For a second Woppit made as if to come toward them, but then the sore on his back must have burned him violently again, because he veered off, tore down into the creek bed nearby, soused himself wildly in a couple of shallow water holes there, and came bounding up the bank again like a maniac.

"Woppit! Woppit!" Turps called, running across the main road to head him off. "Here, Woppit!"

Barnacle stood on his veranda watching the chase. "Must've been more jip in that stuff than I thought," he murmured to himself.

A trailer party had drawn up for lunch on the side of the road by The Big Scrub. There were two cars and two campers. Seven or eight people were moving about preparing lunch. Because it was such a lovely day, they had set up a folding table in the open air. Camp stools were scattered about, a spirit stove was hissing under a billy of water, and food, bottles of sauce, cups, plates, cutlery, and dozens of odds and ends were ready on the table or on the ground nearby. It was a happy picnic scene.

"Woppit! Come back here!" Turps' cry, half angry, half pitying, came to them clearly on the sunny air. They were about to sit down to their meal; a woman was slicing bread and one of the men was bending over the boiling billy, preparing to lift it off to pour the tea.

But at that moment Woppit descended on their camp like a willy-willy.

"Woppit!" Turps' call came too late. The long dingo-colored form swept past the campers, brushed aside camp stools and cartons, shot beneath the table, and leaped over the man at the tea-billy, rising right over his back in a long curving arc that would have done credit to a greyhound. There were shouts and cries on all sides, the collapsible table collapsed, and a sauce bottle smashed against the wheel cap of a trailer in a red splurge.

"Hey!"

"Get out!"

"Blast it!"

"Stop that crazy dog!"

The campers ran out onto the road, but the lean brown arrow of Woppit's body had already shot off through the gates of Bottlebrush Barn and was racing up the track with Turps and Columbine in pursuit.

"What's up with that loony dog? He got rabies or something?" The campers stood muttering angrily. "Better look out. He might come back."

But Woppit wasn't interested in campers, tables, billies, or anything except the burn on his back.

"Woppit! Good dog, Woppit!" Turps' cry went hallooing up the track toward the house, calling and cajoling without effect.

Mrs. Pine was busy staining the front doorstep with blacking. She looked up impatiently as she heard Turps' distant voice.

"What are those two doing now! There isn't time to be playing about with the dogs." She raised her voice. "Crystal! What in the world are you d- . . . *Woppit!*" For Woppit had come plummeting in through the back door and was pounding down the passage toward her. His body was a pudding of mud and dirt, matted lumps of wet fur, bits of grass, bark, and debris, and his paws made long skidding mudprints right down the shining length of the polished linoleum.

Mrs. Pine, kneeling at the front door, saw only a long thundering dog's body, led by a low-hung head, slavering tongue, and staring eyes, hurtling down the passage toward her. "Stop!" she screamed, brandishing the black brush above her head. "Stop!"

Woppit stopped. He dug in his forepaws and skidded down the linoleum, leaving claw marks like furrows and tracing a long muddy wake with the wet mop of his tail. Mrs. Pine saw the ruin of her morning's work behind him.

"Out, you beast!" she shouted. "Out! Out!" And she sprang to her feet and charged at Woppit with the brush. Woppit turned and went to flee down the passage again, but at that moment Turps appeared panting at the back door, calling and yelling his name. Poor Woppit probably thought she wanted to put another dose of fire on his back. He balked and leaped sideways into the living room, normally a holy of holies where dogs were never allowed, and now shining with polished furniture and cozy with freshly brushed rugs. But there the burning itch on his back overcame him again and he rolled furiously on the floor, rubbing his muddy back into the clean pile of the carpet with a kind of desperate relish. Mrs. Pine and Turps discovered him there, lolloping about with his legs in the air and his tongue out.

"Woppit!" They both yelled together, Turps triumphant at having finally cornered him, Mrs. Pine horrified at what was happening to her living room. "Get out!" she screamed. "Get out! Get out! Oh, just look at what he's done to the new white rug!"

Woppit righted himself, shook a shower of mud and water over half the room, and stood at bay, panting like an engine.

"Stand away from the door," Mrs. Pine shouted. "He can't get out!"

Woppit leaped past her, thumping his rump against the door frame as he escaped, and fled for the back door. There he collided with Columbine, almost sending him sprawling for the second time that day, and reached the open air again. There for the next half hour he could be seen rolling about in the yard or rubbing his back against posts and railings. But slowly the burn of the turpentine must have eased and faded, for he behaved less and less spectacularly, and after about an hour he flopped down in a dust hole like a fowl and lay there exhausted.

Mrs. Pine was furious. It took her most of the afternoon to rectify the havoc he'd caused, and even then things were never quite the same again. Turps was both heartbroken and angry—heartbroken at the pain she had accidentally caused Woppit, and angry at Old Barnacle for having suggested such a stupid remedy.

Mr. Pine was inclined to be forgiving when he heard

about it. "I don't think it'll do Woppit any harm," he said. "The old farmers often used to put axle grease or liniment on horses and cows when I was a boy."

"Yes, but Barnacle should have known better."

"He meant it for the best. I wish I could have seen him when Woppit took off."

"He laughed. It was disgusting."

"I'll tell you what was more disgusting," Mrs. Pine said tartly; "my living-room floor after that muddy horse had galloped about in it."

"Wouldn't you gallop too," Mr. Pine replied with a twinkle in his eye, "if someone put turpentine on your tail?"

"Harry!" Mrs. Pine looked at him warningly. But her husband laughed. "Wouldn't you?" "That's enough!" "I'll tell you one thing: I'll bet Woppit won't go near Barnacle again in a hurry."

He was right. Although the old dog's back slowly healed—whether from natural causes or from the turpentine treatment nobody knew—Woppit never again set a paw inside Barnacle's store.

And from that day they always regarded one another from a distance.

Julie
of the Wolves
JEAN CRAIGHEAD GEORGE

Miyax pushed back the hood of her sealskin parka and looked at the Arctic sun. It was a yellow disc in a lime-green sky, the colors of six o'clock in the evening and the time when the wolves awoke. Quietly she put down her cooking pot and crept to the top of a dome-shaped frost heave, one of the many earth buckles that rise and fall in the crackling cold of the Arctic winter. Lying on her stomach, she looked across a vast lawn of grass and moss and focused her attention on the wolves she had come upon two sleeps ago. They were wagging their tails as they awoke and saw each other.

Her hands trembled and her heartbeat quickened, for she was frightened, not so much of the wolves, who were shy and many harpoon-shots away, but because of her desperate predicament. Miyax was lost. She had been lost without food for many sleeps on the North Slope of Alaska. The barren slope stretches for three hundred miles from the Brooks Range to the Arctic Ocean, and for more than eight hundred miles from the Chukchi to the Beaufort Sea. No roads cross it; ponds and lakes freckle its immensity. Winds scream across it, and the view in every direction is exactly the same. Somewhere in this cosmos was Miyax; and the very life in her body, its spark and warmth, depended upon these wolves for survival. And she was not so sure they would help.

Miyax stared hard at the regal black wolf, hoping to catch his eye. She must somehow tell him that she was starving and ask him for food. This could be done she knew, for her father, an Eskimo hunter, had done so. One year he had camped near a wolf den while on a hunt. When a month had passed and her father had seen no game, he told the leader of the wolves that he was hungry and needed food. The next night the wolf called him from far away and her father went to him and found a freshly killed caribou. Unfortunately, Miyax's father never explained to her how he had told the wolf of his needs. And not long afterward he paddled his kayak into the Bering Sea to hunt for seal, and he never returned.

She had been watching the wolves for two days, trying to discern which of their sounds and movements expressed goodwill and friendship. Most animals had such signals. The little Arctic ground squirrels flicked their tails sideways to notify others of their kind that they were friendly. By imitating this signal with her forefinger, Miyax had lured many a squirrel to her hand. If she could discover such a gesture for the wolves she would be able to make friends with them and share their food, like a bird or a fox.

Propped on her elbows with her chin in her fists, she stared at the black wolf, trying to catch his eye. She had chosen him because he was much larger than the others, and because he walked like her father, Kapugen, with his head high and his chest out. The black wolf also possessed wisdom, she had observed. The pack looked to him when the wind carried strange scents or the birds cried nervously. If he was alarmed, they were alarmed. If he was calm, they were calm.

Long minutes passed, and the black wolf did not look at her. He had ignored her since she first came upon them, two sleeps ago. True, she moved slowly and quietly, so as not to alarm him; yet she did wish he would see the kindness in her eyes. Many animals could tell the difference between hostile hunters and friendly people by merely looking at them. But the big black wolf would not even glance her way.

A bird stretched in the grass. The wolf looked at it. A flower twisted in the wind. He glanced at that. Then the breeze rippled the wolverine ruff on Miyax's parka and it glistened in the light. He did not look at that. She waited. Patience with the ways of nature had been instilled in her by her father. And so she knew better than to move or shout. Yet she must get food or die. Her hands shook slightly and she swallowed hard to keep calm.

Miyax was a classic Eskimo beauty, small of bone and delicately wired with strong muscles. Her face was pearl-round and her nose was flat. Her black eyes, which slanted gracefully, were moist and sparkling. Like the beautifully formed polar bears and foxes of the north, she was slightly short-limbed. The frigid environment of the Arctic has sculptured life into compact shapes. Unlike the long-limbed, long-bodied animals of the south that are cooled by dispensing heat on extended surfaces, all live things in the Arctic tend toward compactness, to conserve heat.

The length of her limbs and the beauty of her face were of no use to Miyax as she lay on the lichen-speckled frost heave in the midst of the bleak tundra. Her stomach ached and the royal black wolf was carefully ignoring her.

"*Amaroq, ilaya,* wolf, my friend," she finally called. "Look at me. Look at me."

She spoke half in Eskimo and half in English, as if the instincts of her father and the science of the *gussaks,* the white-faced, might evoke some magical combination that would help her get her message through to the wolf.

Amaroq glanced at his paw and slowly turned his head her way without lifting his eyes. He licked his shoulder. A few matted hairs sprang apart and twinkled individually. Then his eyes sped to each of the three adult wolves that made up his pack and finally to the five pups who were sleeping in a fuzzy mass near the den entrance. The great wolf's eyes softened at the sight of the little wolves, then quickly hardened into brittle yellow jewels as he scanned the flat tundra.

Not a tree grew anywhere to break the monotony of the gold-green plain, for the soils of the tundra are permanently frozen. Only moss, grass, lichens, and a few hardy flowers take root in the thin upper layer that thaws briefly in summer. Nor do many species of animals live in this rigorous land, but those creatures that do dwell here exist in bountiful numbers. Amaroq watched a large cloud of Lapland longspurs wheel up into the sky, then alight in the grasses. Swarms of crane flies, one of the few insects that can survive the cold, darkened the tips of the mosses. Birds wheeled, turned, and called. Thousands sprang up from the ground like leaves in a wind.

The wolf's ears cupped forward and tuned in on some distant message from the tundra. Miyax tensed and listened, too. Did he hear some brewing storm, some approaching enemy? Apparently not. His ears relaxed and he rolled to his side. She sighed, glanced at the vaulting sky, and was painfully aware of her predicament.

Here she was, watching wolves—she, Miyax, daughter of Kapugen, adopted child of Martha, citizen of the United States, pupil at the Bureau of Indian Affairs School in Barrow, Alaska, and thirteen-year-old wife of the boy Daniel. She shivered at the thought of Daniel, for it was he who had driven her to this fate. She had run away from him exactly seven sleeps ago, and because of this she had one more title by gussak standards—the child divorcée.

The wolf rolled to his belly.

"Amaroq," she whispered. "I am lost and the sun will not set for a month. There is no North Star to guide me."

Amaroq did not stir.

"And there are no berry bushes here to bend under the polar wind and point to the south. Nor are there any birds I can follow." She looked up. "Here the birds are buntings and longspurs. They do not fly to the sea twice a day like the puffins and sandpipers that my father followed."

The wolf groomed his chest with his tongue.

"I never dreamed I could get lost, Amaroq," she went on, talking out loud to ease her fear. "At home on Nunivak Island where I was born, the plants and birds pointed the way for wanderers. I thought they did so everywhere . . . and so, great black Amaroq, I'm without a compass."

It had been a frightening moment when two days ago she realized that the tundra was an ocean of grass on which she was circling around and around. Now as that fear overcame her again she closed her eyes. When she opened them her heart skipped excitedly. Amaroq was looking at her!

"Ee-lie," she called and scrambled to her feet. The

wolf arched his neck and narrowed his eyes. He pressed his ears forward. She waved. He drew back his lips and showed his teeth. Frightened by what seemed a snarl, she lay down again. When she was flat on her stomach, Amaroq flattened his ears and wagged his tail once. Then he tossed his head and looked away.

Discouraged, she wriggled backward down the frost heave and arrived at her camp feet first. The heave was between herself and the wolf pack and so she relaxed, stood up, and took stock of her home. It was a simple affair, for she had not been able to carry much when she ran away; she took just those things she would need for the journey—a backpack, food for a week or so, needles to mend clothes, matches, her sleeping skin, and ground cloth to go under it, two knives, and a pot.

She had intended to walk to Point Hope. There she would meet the *North Star*, the ship that brings supplies from the States to the towns on the Arctic Ocean in August when the ice pack breaks up. The ship could always use dishwashers or laundresses, she had heard, and so she would work her way to San Francisco where Amy, her pen pal, lived. At the end of every letter Amy always wrote: "When are you coming to San Francisco?" Seven days ago she had been on her way—on her way to the glittering, white, postcard city that sat on a hill among trees, those enormous plants she had never seen.

She had been on her way to see the television and carpeting in Amy's school, the glass buildings, traffic lights, and stores full of fruits; on her way to the harbor that never froze and the Golden Gate Bridge. But primarily she was on her way to be rid of Daniel, her terrifying husband.

She kicked the sod at the thought of her marriage; then shaking her head to forget, she surveyed her camp. It was nice. Upon discovering the wolves, she had settled down to live near them in the hope of sharing their food, until the sun set and the stars came out to guide her. She had built a house of sod, like the summer homes of the old Eskimos. Each brick had been cut with her *ulo*, the half-moon shaped woman's knife, so versatile it can trim a baby's hair, slice a tough bear, or chip an iceberg.

Her house was not well built for she had never made one before, but it was cozy inside. She had windproofed it by sealing the sod bricks with mud from the pond at her door, and she had made it beautiful by spreading her caribou ground cloth on the floor. On this she had placed her sleeping skin, a moosehide bag lined with soft white rabbit skins. Next to her bed she had built a low table of sod on which to put her clothes when she slept. To decorate the house she had made three flowers of bird feathers and stuck them in the top of the table.

Then she had built a fireplace outdoors and placed her pot beside it. The pot was empty, for she had not found even a lemming to eat. . . .

Unfortunately for Miyax, the hour of the animals that prey on the lemmings was also over. The white fox, the snowy owl, the weasel, the jaeger, and the siskin had virtually disappeared. They had no food to eat and bore few or no young. Those that lived preyed on each other. With the passing of the lemmings, however, the grasses had grown high again and the hour of the caribou was upon the land. Healthy fat caribou cows gave birth to many calves. The caribou population increased, and this in turn increased the number of wolves who prey on the caribou. The abundance of the big deer of the north did Miyax no good, for she had not brought a gun on her trip. It had never occurred to her that she would not reach Point Hope before her food ran out.

A dull pain seized her stomach. She pulled blades of grass from their sheaths and ate the sweet ends. They were not very satisfying, so she picked a handful of caribou moss, a lichen. If the deer could survive in winter on this food, why not she? She munched, decided the plant might taste better if cooked, and went to the pond for water.

As she dipped her pot in, she thought about Amaroq. Why had he bared his teeth at her? Because she was young and he knew she couldn't hurt him? No, she said to herself, it was because he was speaking to her! He had told her to lie down. She had even understood and obeyed him. He had talked to her not with his voice, but with his ears, eyes, and lips; and he had even commended her with a wag of his tail.

She dropped her pot, scrambled up the frost heave and stretched out on her stomach.

"Amaroq," she called softly, "I understand what you said. Can you understand me? I'm hungry—very, very hungry. Please bring me some meat."

The great wolf did not look her way and she began to doubt her reasoning. After all, flattened ears and a tail-wag were scarcely a conversation. She dropped her forehead against the lichens and rethought what had gone between them.

"Then why did I lie down?" she asked, lifting her head and looking at Amaroq. "Why did I?" she called to the yawning wolves. Not one turned her way.

Amaroq got to his feet, and as he slowly arose he seemed to fill the sky and blot out the sun. He was enormous. He could swallow her without even chewing.

"But he won't," she reminded herself. "Wolves do not eat people. That's gussak talk. Kapugen said wolves are gentle brothers."

The black puppy was looking at her and wagging his tail. Hopefully, Miyax held out a pleading hand to him. His tail wagged harder. The mother rushed to him and stood above him sternly. When he licked her cheek apologetically, she pulled back her lips from her fine white teeth. They flashed as she smiled and forgave her cub.

"But don't let it happen again," said Miyax sarcastically, mimicking her own elders. The mother walked toward Amaroq.

"I should call you Martha after my stepmother," Miyax whispered. "But you're much too beautiful. I shall call you Silver instead."

Silver moved in a halo of light, for the sun sparkled on the guard hairs that grew out over the dense underfur and she seemed to glow. . . .

Amaroq was pacing restlessly along the crest of the frost heave as if something were about to happen. His eyes shot to Silver, then to the gray wolf Miyax had named Nails. These glances seemed to be a summons, for Silver and Nails glided to him, spanked the ground with their forepaws and bit him gently under the chin. He wagged his tail furiously and took Silver's slender nose in his mouth. She crouched before him, licked his cheek and lovingly bit his lower jaw. Amaroq's tail flashed high as her mouthing charged him with vitality. He nosed her affectionately. Unlike the fox who met his mate only in the breeding season, Amaroq lived with his mate all year.

Next, Nails took Amaroq's jaw in his mouth and the leader bit the top of his nose. A third adult, a small male,

came slinking up. He got down on his belly before Amaroq, rolled trembling to his back, and wriggled.

"Hello, Jello," Miyax whispered, for he reminded her
of the quivering gussak dessert her mother-in-law made.

She had seen the wolves mouth Amaroq's chin twice
before and so she concluded that it was a ceremony, a
sort of "Hail to the Chief." He must indeed be their
leader for he was clearly the wealthy wolf; that is, wealthy
as she had known the meaning of the word on Nunivak
Island. There the old Eskimo hunters she had known in
her childhood thought the riches of life were intelligence,
fearlessness, and love. A man with these gifts was rich
and was a great spirit who was admired in the same
way that the gussaks admired a man with money and
goods. . . .

Any fear Miyax had of the wolves was dispelled by
their affection for each other. They were friendly animals
and so devoted to Amaroq that she needed only to be
accepted by him to be accepted by all. She even knew
how to achieve this—bite him under the chin. But how
was she going to do that?

She studied the pups hoping they had a simpler way
of expressing their love for him. The black puppy approached the leader, sat, then lay down and wagged his
tail vigorously. He gazed up at Amaroq in pure adora-
tion, and the royal eyes softened. . . .

Miyax hunched forward on her elbows, the better to

see and learn. She now knew how to be a good puppy, pay tribute to the leader, and even to be a leader by biting others on the top of the nose. She also knew how to tell Jello to baby-sit. If only she had big ears and a tail, she could lecture and talk to them all.

Flapping her hands on her head for ears, she flattened her fingers to make friends, pulled them together and back to express fear, and shot them forward to display her aggression and dominance. Then she folded her arms and studied the puppies again.

The black one greeted Jello by tackling his feet. Another jumped on his tail, and before he could discipline either, all five were upon him. He rolled and tumbled with them for almost an hour; then he ran down the slope, turned, and stopped. The pursuing pups plowed into him, tumbled, fell, and lay still. During a minute of surprised recovery there was no action. Then the black pup flashed his tail like a semaphore signal and they all jumped on Jello again.

Miyax rolled over and laughed aloud. "That's funny. They're really like kids."

When she looked back, Jello's tongue was hanging from his mouth and his sides were heaving. Four of the puppies had collapsed at his feet and were asleep. Jello flopped down, too, but the black pup still looked around. He was not the least bit tired. Miyax watched him, for there was something special about him.

He ran to the top of the den and barked. The smallest pup, whom Miyax called Sister, lifted her head, saw her favorite brother in action and, struggling to her feet, followed him devotedly. While they romped, Jello took the opportunity to rest behind a clump of sedge, a moisture-loving plant of the tundra. But hardly was he settled before a pup tracked him to his hideout and pounced on him. Jello narrowed his eyes, pressed his ears forward, and showed his teeth.

"I know what you're saying," she called to him. "You're saying, 'lie down.'" The puppy lay down, and Miyax got on all fours and looked for the nearest pup to speak to. It was Sister.

"Ummmm," she whined, and when Sister turned around she narrowed her eyes and showed her white teeth. Obediently, Sister lay down.

"I'm talking wolf! I'm talking wolf!" Miyax clapped, and tossing her head like a pup, crawled in a happy circle. As she was coming back she saw all five puppies sitting in a row watching her, their heads cocked in curiosity. Boldly the black pup came toward her, his fat backside swinging as he trotted to the bottom of her frost heave, and barked.

"You are *very* fearless and *very* smart," she said. "Now I know why you are special. You are wealthy and the leader of the puppies. There is no doubt what you'll grow up to be. So I shall name you after my father Kapugen, and I shall call you Kapu for short."

Kapu wrinkled his brow and turned an ear to tune in more acutely on her voice.

"You don't understand, do you?"

Hardly had she spoken than his tail went up, his mouth opened slightly, and he fairly grinned.

"Ee-lie!" she gasped. "You do understand. And that scares me." She perched on her heels. Jello whined an undulating note and Kapu turned back to the den.

Miyax imitated the call to come home. Kapu looked back over his shoulder in surprise. She giggled. He wagged his tail and jumped on Jello.

She clapped her hands and settled down to watch this language of jumps and tumbles, elated that she was at last breaking the wolf code. After a long time she decided they were not talking but roughhousing, and so she started home. Later she changed her mind. Roughhousing was very important to wolves. It occupied almost the entire night for the pups.

"Ee-lie, okay," she said. "I'll learn to roughhouse. Maybe then you'll accept me and feed me." She pranced, jumped, and whimpered; she growled, snarled, and rolled. But nobody came to roughhouse.

Sliding back to her camp, she heard the grass swish and looked up to see Amaroq and his hunters sweep around her frost heave and stop about five feet away. She could smell the sweet scent of their fur.

The hairs on her neck rose and her eyes widened. Amaroq's ears went forward aggressively and she remembered that wide eyes meant fear to him. It was not good to show him she was afraid. Animals attacked the fearful. She tried to narrow them, but remembered that was not right either. Narrowed eyes were mean. In desperation she recalled that Kapu had moved forward when challenged. She pranced right up to Amaroq. Her heart beat furiously as she grunt-whined the sound of the puppy begging adoringly for attention. Then she got down on her belly and gazed at him with fondness.

The great wolf backed up and avoided her eyes. She had said something wrong! Perhaps even offended him. Some slight gesture that meant nothing to her had apparently meant something to the wolf. His ears shot forward angrily and it seemed all was lost. She wanted to get up and run, but she gathered her courage and pranced closer to him. Swiftly she patted him under the chin.

The signal went off. It sped through his body and triggered emotions of love. Amaroq's ears flattened and his tail wagged in friendship. He could not react in any other way to the chin pat, for the roots of this signal lay deep in wolf history. It was inherited from generations and generations of leaders before him. As his eyes softened, the sweet odor of ambrosia arose from the gland on the top of his tail and she was drenched lightly in wolf scent. Miyax was one of the pack. . . .

> *Nevertheless, the wolves brought her no food that night, so she ate cold raw moss, crawled into the cozy hut she had built, thought about the wolves and went to sleep.*

Miyax did not know how long she slept, for midnight was almost as bright as noon and it was difficult to judge the passing of time. It did not matter, however; time in the Arctic was the rhythm of life. The wolf pups were barking their excited *yipoo* that rang out the hour of the end of the hunt. The pack was coming home. With visions of caribou stew in her head, she got out of her sleeping skin and reached for her clothes. . . .

Quickly she climbed the frost heave, lay down, and looked at the wolves. There was no meat to be seen. The three hunters were stretched out on their sides, their bellies extended with food. Jello was gone. Of course, she said to herself, he had been relieved of his duties and had backtracked the hunters to the kill. She winced, for she had been so certain that today she would eat. So I won't, she said to herself, and that's that.

Miyax knew when to stop dreaming and be practical. She slid down the heave, brushed off her parka, and faced the tundra. The plants around the pond had edible seeds, as did all of the many grasses. There were thousands of crane fly and mosquito larvae in the water, and the wildflowers were filling if not very nourishing. But they were all small and took time to gather. She looked around for something bigger. . . .

A movement in the sky above the horizon caught her attention, and she recognized the pointed tail and black head of a jaeger. She knew this bird well, for it hunted the shore and tundra of Nunivak Island. A bold sea bird, it resembled its close relative the gull, but was not a fisher. The jaeger preyed upon lemmings, small birds, and occasionally carrion. Miyax wondered what prey it was hunting. Three more jaegers joined the first, circled close together as if over a target, then dropped out of sight below the horizon.

"The wolf kill!" she fairly shouted. "They're sharing the wolf kill."

Jumping to her feet, she lined up the spot where they had disappeared with a patch of brown lichens in the distance, and ran with joy along the invisible line. When she had gone a quarter of a mile, she stopped and looked back. The endless tundra rolled around her and she could not tell which frost heave was which.

"Oh, no!" she cried. She turned around and laboriously searched out the plants crushed by her feet. Near a pool she lost all sight of her steps and then with relief recognized an empty lemming nest, a round ball of grass that she had kicked open. She pounced on it, saw a flower she had trampled, and ran up the heave to it. From the top she looked across the distance to her own precious house.

She reminded herself not to be so careless again. "One can get lost out here," she said aloud. . . .

Silver came up the long slope, gave the grunt-whine that summoned the pups, and Kapu ran to meet her. She pulled back her lips in a smile and nosed him affectionately. Then Kapu stuck his nose in the corner of her mouth. Silver arched her back, her neck rippled, and she choked up a big mound of meat. Kapu set upon it with a snarl.

"So that's it!" said Miyax. "The meat's in the belly-basket. Now what do I do?"

Kapu let Sister share the meal with him, but not Zing, Zat, and Zit—as Miyax had dubbed the three tawny pups who had little personality as yet. Zing rushed over to the resting Silver and cuddled up against her. He rammed his nose against her teats and taking one in his mouth, ravenously nursed. Silver tolerated this for a moment, then growled. He did not let go and she snapped at him. He pulled away, but when she stretched out he dove back into her belly fur again. With a loud bark she rolled onto her stomach and cut off her milk from him. Zing got up, walked over to Amaroq, and stuck his nose in the corner of his mouth. Amaroq regurgitated food.

The secret of the fat pups was out. They were being weaned from mother's milk to well-chewed and partially digested food.

They might eat food from the belly-basket for weeks before they were brought chunks of meat that Miyax could share, and so she went out into the grasses again to look for buntings. Soon Silver and Nails trotted off in the direction of the kill. Having fed the puppies, they were now feeding themselves. Miyax cautiously peered around the heave. Jello had not gone with them. Yet he had been to the kill. He would have food in his belly-basket.

When the jaegers arose into the air she picked up the pot and climbed once again to the top of her frost heave. Getting to her hands and knees, she gave the grunt-whine call. "Look at me. I'm nice," it said.

Jello strode toward her. So pushed around was he by Silver, so respectful of Amaroq and even Nails, that he was excited by a voice more humble than his own. He even lifted his tail and head higher than Miyax had ever seen him do, and, acting like the boss wolf, loped up her frost heave. Curious Kapu trotted behind.

As Miyax scurried to meet Jello, he hesitated, growled softly, and urinated. "Don't be scared," she said and whimpered. He circled closer. Quickly rising to her knees, grunting the note of friendship, she slipped her hand over his head and clasped the top of his nose firmly in her fingers.

"I'm boss," she said as his tail and head went down in deference to the symbol of leadership. She started to slip her hand into the corner of his mouth, but he jerked away. Then Kapu, as if he understood what Miyax wanted, swept up to Jello and nuzzled his mouth. Jello heaved, opened his jaws, and deposited food on the ground.

"I'll live! I'll live!" Miyax cried jubilantly as Jello turned, put his tail between his legs, and raced back to the other pups. Kapu sat down and watched with wrinkled forehead as she scooped the meat into the pot. When she had retrieved every morsel, she gently closed her lips on the bridge of his nose. His tail wagged respectfully and he gazed softly into her eyes.

"Kapu," she whispered, "we Eskimos have joking partners—people to have fun with—and serious partners—people to work and think with. You and I are both. We are joking-serious partners." He wagged his tail excitedly and blinked. "And that's the best of all."

The Black Pearl

SCOTT O'DELL

Sixteen-year-old Ramon Salazar is learning to be a partner in his father's pearl-fishing business. He has heard all his life of the dreaded Manta Diablo, the huge and vicious sea creature that threatens the safety of pearl divers off the coast of Baja California. Taunted in secret by "the Sevillano," champion diver in his father's fleet, Ramon is determined to find for himself a pearl so great it will win him fabulous fame.

red haze hung over the water as I floated the canoe on the morning of the fourth day and began to paddle toward the cave where the old man said the Manta Diablo lived.

The sun was up but the haze hung so thick that I had trouble locating the channel. After I found it I searched for almost an hour before I sighted the cave. It was hidden behind a rocky pinnacle and faced the rising sun, and the opening was about thirty feet wide and the height of a tall man, and curved downward like the upper lip of a mouth. I could not see into the cave because of the red mist, so I drifted back and forth and waited until the sun rose higher and the mist burned away.

I had talked to the old man the night before about the cave. We had eaten supper, and the women and children had gone to bed, and the two of us were sitting around the fire.

"You have fished everywhere in the lagoon," I said, "but not in the cave."

"No," he said. "Nor did my father nor his father."

"Big pearls may grow there."

The old man did not answer. He got up and put wood on the fire and sat down again.

"The great one itself, the Pearl of Heaven, may lie there," I said.

Still he did not answer, but suddenly he looked across the fire. It was a fleeting look that he gave me and yet its meaning was as clear as if he had spoken to me and said, "I cannot go to the cave to search for pearls. I cannot go because I fear the Manta Diablo. If you go there, then it is alone. El Diablo cannot blame me."

And that morning when I went down to the beach he did not go with me. "The wound on my hand hurts very much," he said, "so I will stay behind." And the look he gave me was the same I had seen the night before.

At last, about midmorning, the sun burned away the mist and I could see for a short distance into the cave. I paddled through the mouth and soon found myself in a vast vault-like room. The walls of the room were black and smooth and shone from the light that came in through the opening.

Near the mouth of the cave the water was very clear. I picked up my basket and sink stone, took a deep breath, and slipped over the side of the canoe, remembering all that the old man had taught me.

I reached the bottom after about a fathom and a half. I looped my foot in the rope tied to the sink stone and waited until the bubbles that had risen behind me disappeared and I could find the bed of shells I had noticed from above. The bed was five steps away toward the mouth of the cave. I walked carefully in the sand as I had learned to do.

The shells were the largest I had ever seen. They were half the length of my arm and thick through as my body and covered with weed that looked like a woman's hair. I chose the nearest one, which seemed to be easier to get at than the others. I took out my knife and worked quietly, but a school of small fish kept swimming in front of my eyes, so I failed to pry the shell loose before my lungs began to hurt and I had to go up.

On my second dive I had no sooner reached the bottom than a shadow fell across the bed where I was working. It was the shadow of a gray shark, one of the friendly ones, but by the time he had drifted away my breath was gone.

I dived six times more and worked quickly each time I went down, hacking away with my sharp knife at the base of the big shell where it was anchored to the rock. But it had been growing there for many years, since long before I was born, I suppose, and it would not come free from its home.

By this time it was late in the afternoon and the light was poor. Also my hands were bleeding and my eyes were half-blind with salt from the sea. But I sat in the canoe and thought of all the hours I had spent for nothing. And I thought too of the Sevillano and the great pearl he had found, or said he had found, in the Gulf of Persia.

I filled my lungs and took the sink stone and went down again. With the first stroke of my knife, the shell came free. It toppled over on one side, and I quickly untied the rope from the sink stone and looped it twice around the shell and swam back to the surface. I pulled up the shell, but it was too heavy for me to lift into the canoe, so I tied it to the stern and paddled out of the cave.

Across the lagoon I could see the old man standing among the trees. From time to time during the day I had caught glimpses of him standing there with his eyes fixed on the cave. I knew that I could drown and he would not try to save me, and that he was telling El Diablo all the while that he had not wanted me to go to the cave and that he therefore was not to blame. But I also felt that if I found a pearl he would be willing to take his share because he had nothing to do with finding it.

He came out from the trees as I paddled across the lagoon and strolled down to the beach as if he did not care whether I had found a pearl or not. I suppose this was to show El Diablo and his friends the fish and the long, gray shark that Soto Luzon was without blame.

"A big one," he said when I dragged the shell ashore. "In my life I have never seen such a monster. It is the grandfather of all oysters that live in the sea."

"There are many in the cave bigger than this one," I said.

"If there are so many," he answered, "then the Manta

Diablo cannot be mad that you have taken only one of them."

"Perhaps a little mad," I said and laughed, "but not much."

The mouth of the oyster was closed and it was hard to put my blade between the tight edges of the shell.

"Lend me your knife," I said. "Mine is blunted from use."

The old man placed his hand on the hilt of his knife and pulled it from the sheath and then slipped it back again.

"I think it is better if you use your own knife," he said and his voice began to tremble as he spoke.

I wrestled a long time with the oyster. At last the hard lips began to give a little. Then I could feel the knife sink through the heavy muscles that held them together and suddenly the lips fell apart.

I put my finger under the frilled edge of the flesh as I had seen my father do. A pearl slid along my finger and I picked it out. It was about the size of a pea. When I felt again, another of the same size rolled out and then a third. I put them on the other half of the shell so they would not be scratched.

The old man came and leaned over me, as I knelt there in the sand, and held his breath.

Slowly I slid my hand under the heavy tongue of the oyster. I felt a hard lump, so monstrous in size that it could not be a pearl. I took hold of it and pulled it from the flesh and got to my feet and held it to the sun, thinking that I must be holding a rock that the oyster had swallowed somehow.

It was round and smooth and the color of smoke. It filled my cupped hand. Then the sun's light struck deep into the thing and moved in silver swirls and I knew that it was not a rock that I held but a pearl, the great Pearl of Heaven.

"Madre de Dios," the old man whispered.

I stood there and could not move or talk. The old man kept whispering over and over, "Madre de Dios."

Darkness fell. I tore off the tail of my shirt and wrapped the pearl in it.

"Half of this is yours," I told him.

I handed the pearl to him, but he drew back in fear.

"You wish me to keep it until we reach La Paz?" I said.

"Yes, it is better that you keep it."

"When shall we go?"

"Soon," he said hoarsely. "El Diablo is away but he will come back. And his friends will tell him then about the pearl."

The Bushbabies
WILLIAM STEVENSON

*Thirteen-year-old Jacqueline Rhodes,
having lived most of her life in the game
preserve in Kenya where her father has
been Warden, regrets leaving Africa for
home in England. An accident separates
her and her dearly loved "bushbaby,"
a furry galago, from her family; and
Jackie feels she must return her pet,
Kamau, to its native forest before she
tries to rejoin her family. She enlists the
help of her father's black former servant,
Tembo. However, a newscast she hears
on her father's portable radio reveals she
has endangered the life of the elderly
native, for Nairobi authorities believe he*

has kidnapped her and have issued orders to shoot him on sight. Having sheltered overnight in her family's remote riverside vacation cabin, Jackie believes she and Tembo can successfully complete their trek across East African forest, hunting for food as they dodge the expected rains.

efore she closed up the cottage again, Jackie unhooked a copy of an old map left hanging in a back room. Her father had kept the original, drawn by a young British naval lieutenant and still bearing his faded signature. It was dated 1882 and it recorded the known trails followed by the Arab slaving caravans.

"This man hunted the Arab slavers."

Tembo's face lit up. "Who was this man?"

Proudly she deciphered the name. "John Flaxman." She knew exactly what kind of man he was. There was a very dogeared photograph of him in later life, among her mother's mementos. John Flaxman had been her grandfather.

"Wa!" said Tembo. "He must have killed many slavers."

"His job was chasing them into the mangrove swamps in the mouths of the rivers. Sometimes the Arabs laid traps and jumped upon the naval boats."

Flaxman had recorded some of these adventures on the back of the chart. The photocopy faithfully reproduced the ink, faded to a faint brown wriggle, and the way the paper had been creased and fly-blown. The map still showed in useful detail the lower reaches of the river on which they planned to sail.

"We can—borrow—a canoe here," she said. "And catch some fish before going upriver." She salved her conscience with the reflection that John Flaxman would not have scrupled to steal a canoe in a good cause.

She drew great comfort from the chart. She remembered her mother's stories of how Flaxman had risked an early death from malaria or an Arab muzzle-loader, and it seemed almost as if he were marching right beside her.

They struck out first toward the northeast, the man in his fiber cloak and battered askari's kepi, his big feet bare; and the girl in jodhpurs and whipcord jacket, and the boots made from the ear of an elephant. Their path lay through a sprawling plantation of sisal. They walked single file between the rows of gray-green spears. Here and there the sisal plants had been allowed to "pole." Instead of a bunch of stiff needle-pointed leaves clustered like cacti, there soared tall knotted stems with puffs or seedpods at the top.

Few people were abroad. Near the estate's water tower, marking the manager's house, voices could be heard. A few sisal workers clustered around a truck on the Mombasa road. Tembo gave them all a wide berth; and shortly they came to the mouth of the river.

A big old baobab sheltered them from view. The tree was fat and gray, with huge warts and goiters, and its branches were like the roots of an upturned carrot. The man and the girl rested their loads against this venerable tree, and took stock.

In normal times the river was a good half-mile wide. The drought had reduced it considerably. Midstream floated several *ngalawas*, the outrigger canoes used by fishermen. Jackie examined them greedily. Which one would carry them upriver?

The canoes were equipped with large white dagger sails, also borrowed from the Arabs whose dhows came down this coast before the November monsoon. For centuries past, the crescent sails were to be seen poised on the horizon like a flock of birds; and in the holds of the dhows came dried fish and Mangalore tiles, carpets, and camphorwood chests.

Jackie studied the little canoes, a crude blend of Arab and African tradition. Not long ago, as she knew from the notes on John Flaxman's map, this place had been the base of an Arab slave route. *"The caravans march inland,"* Flaxman had written in his tiny copperplate hand. *"Each is made up of hundreds of white-clad Arabs under the red flag of the Sultan . . . The captured slaves are roped together in single file, each slave's neck in a forked stick about six feet long supported on the shoulders of the slave in front—flogged along the forest paths with rawhide whips."*

The girl shivered. In the early morning light it was easy to imagine the ghosts of slaves passing through the shafts of green that penetrated the forest beside the river.

"We must steal one of the canoes," she said, interrupting her own thoughts. "Later we can arrange for its return."

"Yes," said Tembo. His mind must have been pursuing a similar course to Jackie's earlier thoughts, however, because he added: "It is always possible to trace the Arab slave routes by following the line of the old mango trees."

She gave him a startled look. It had never occurred to her that a Kamba warrior would have such a strong memory of slaving days.

"Why?"

Tembo shrugged and held out the palms of his hands. "Perhaps the Arabs brought the mango here in the first place. Perhaps they took mangoes on the long marches

187

inland, and scattered the seeds. It is a saying of many Africans here. The mango tree is the footprint of the slaver."

Struck by an idea, Jackie fished out the old map. Sure enough, Flaxman had marked a slave route starting at this very point. It ran alongside the river to just about where Jackie and the man had agreed they would have to turn inland and travel on foot.

"Look," she said excitedly. "There was a slave route from here—" She spread the map on the baked earth. "—to here." Her finger found the intersection of the Mombasa railroad and the dirt highway to Nairobi. It was less than a couple of miles from Ndi, their destination.

"Which means," she said slowly, "when we leave the river, we can check our direction by the mango trees. If," she added, "they're still there."

Tembo pointed a few yards up the river, where the bank sloped steeply to the sluggish waters. A dark mango tree towered above the bananas whose huge torn leaves drooped like tattered wings.

"I think the mangoes will be always with us," he said sadly.

The girl thought it strange and terrible that the mango should represent, for Africans like Tembo, the dreadful years when thousands were torn from their native villages to be sold into the most vicious forms of slavery.

And yet it was natural for Africans to view the alien tree with suspicion. For the mango was not native to Africa. Its tiny pink and fragrant flowers were more familiar to Buddha and the people of Asia, from where they came. The mango flowers, thought Jackie, were like a trail of blood. The Arabs who dropped the seeds had unwittingly left a permanent record of their bloody raids.

"I must stop dreaming," said Jackie aloud.

The old man smiled. "It is better sometimes to stand and dream than to engage in futile action." He pointed downstream where the white roots of the mangrove trees stretched like spiders' legs into the estuary. Around the western cape, advancing toward them, chugged a coast-guard launch.

"Gosh!" Jackie snatched up Kamau's basket. "They might have caught us stealing . . ."

The launch moved slowly upstream. When it was almost abreast, Jackie saw a uniformed figure in the bows studying both banks through binoculars. It occurred to her that the object of this search might be Tembo, but she kept this disquieting thought to herself. Instead, she flattened herself against the trunk of the baobab tree and waited for the launch to vanish from sight.

The river was so quiet that long after the launch had gone they could hear its wake ripple against the banks.

"We must take the canoe now," said Tembo. "Before the fishermen begin to stir."

"Suppose the launch returns?"

"You must keep out of sight. Let us hope nobody looks too closely."

Each canoe was tied to a mangrove pole. Warped planks of wood were lashed to the poles, forming a rough kind of jetty. Tembo inched gingerly along the planks above the shallow muddy water until he found a canoe to his taste. He returned with it, maneuvering with a paddle shaped at the bottom like a water-lily leaf.

He steered the canoe under the vegetation that spilled over the bank at Jackie's feet. She lowered their packs first, hugging Kamau's basket before jumping down last of all.

The hull of the canoe was deep and narrow, carved from the trunk of a single tree. It would have overbalanced except for the outriggers, two pairs of horizontal poles lashed to bow and stern at right angles to the hull. A crudely carved plank ran lengthwise at the extremity of each pair of outriggers, so that when the canoe rolled there was always a stabilizing counter-action from one of the planks.

"Where did you learn to canoe?"

"I was an askari on an expedition to Lake Rudolph. We were many weeks on the water in dugouts." He used the Swahili word "*ngalawa*." The girl liked the word. She liked speaking Swahili. It was a simple language but in the man's mouth it had a considerable dignity.

They paddled first beyond the river's mouth, turning eastward along the coast a short way. Tembo had lost some of his inherent dislike of the sea itself, and watched eagerly as the girl maneuvered them above the coral. There was a rope, weighted with a rock, that served as an anchor. This she lowered until it lodged in the nigger-head.

"We must not stay long," he warned.

"Ten minutes," she promised, snapping on the goggles and taking a speargun. "There are many fish here, and easy to catch."

"Perhaps I could try?"

"Of course!" Her eyes lit up. "You can hang onto the canoe's side, and rest your feet on the coral."

She picked up a speargun and showed him how to use it. As so often happened, she found Swahili a limiting language in which to explain technicalities. And yet it forced a simplicity of phrase that made her think more clearly.

The speargun was a two-foot stick bleached white by sun and sea. Near the thick butt was a second piece of wood, secured like a peg by stout rubber bands. A piece of straight thick wire, fashioned into a crude arrow, lay in a groove along the top of the speargun. A notch had been cut in the back of this rough harpoon.

"You load it this way," said Jackie, putting the butt of the gun against her chest and pulling back a hunk of powerful elastic. Where the rubber looped, wire had been twisted protectively around it and was now engaged in the notch of the harpoon. "You clip it like this." She adjusted the wooden peg so it gripped the end of the harpoon.

It was a simple device. Tembo saw that if you depressed the peg, the wire harpoon would be flung a short distance. There was a light piece of nylon fishing line that secured the harpoon to the swimmer, to prevent the escape of an injured fish. His love of the hunt was aroused and he fingered the gun with lively curiosity.

"Let's go!" Jackie picked up the second harpoon and lowered herself over the side of the canoe. Tembo followed her, and found that he could balance on the niggerhead by leaning against one of the canoe's outriggers.

"What about Kamau?" he shouted, catching sight of the bushbaby creeping out of the basket.

But Jackie was already stalking a flat, diamond-shaped creature moving slowly across a bed of sand. It was a sand-gray plaice, propelling itself with the graceful undulations of a large bird. She sighted along the speargun and fired. Her eyes, magnified by the goggles, gleamed triumphantly. The little harpoon, still attached to her wrist by the line, had pinned the fish to the seabed.

She surfaced, took a deep breath, and dived to retrieve the speared fish. On her way down she had unhitched the knife at her waist, and she hacked through the foremost point of the fish where two closely placed eyes peered helplessly up at her. Then she grabbed the harpoon with her free hand and shot back to the surface, the dying fish flapping on the harpoon's barb.

"It is small but good to eat," she said, swimming back to the canoe and tossing the fish into the bottom.

She caught sight of Kamau, who was squatting on the prow. His ears were pinned back and he regarded the fish with evident distaste, uttering a cry of distress that sounded like the twanging of a guitar string.

"Will he be safe?" asked Tembo.

"Yes." The girl spoke with conviction. "He fears water."

She dived back under the sea.

Tembo squinted at the bushbaby. He seemed to be frozen to his perch, and it was unlikely that he would move. The man smiled to himself at the way in which Jackie had become immersed in the excitement of pursuing her prey. It was something Tembo understood very well.

Holding the outrigger with one hand, he sank below the sea's surface, peering through the goggles Jackie had given him.

Almost at once a large sea bass, a grouper, swam lazily into his vision, its huge mouth agape.

Tembo lifted his head and gulped a great lungful of air. When he ducked under again, the grouper had swum so close that it seemed enormous. Shakily he aimed the speargun and fired.

To his surprise and delight, the harpoon struck the grouper in one of its unblinking eyes. The fish seemed to become fiery red and turned tail in a flash, almost jerking the harpoon line from Tembo's hand. He staggered back, astonished by the weight of its pull. The grouper threshed back and forth on the end of the line and then dived for a hole in another arched cathedral of coral.

The man's excited shouts now brought Jackie splashing to his side. She yelled instructions to keep the line taut, and dived for the hole.

He saw her sink slowly down the side of the nigger-head, saw the grouper peer at her from the darkness of the hole, and then watched in horror as an unspeakably grotesque creature like a fat and wart-ridden snake reared up from an adjoining cavity.

Tembo tried to cry a warning but water clogged his throat. He vomited, caught his breath, and ducked once more under water. His hand gripping the outrigger shook violently.

The girl had thrust her arm into the grouper's retreat. Gripping it by the gills, she hauled the struggling fish into open water.

Behind her the creature resembling a snake emerged clear from its hole. It was a good five feet in length, with a crinkly green head and gaping jaws sewn with teeth. The body was smooth and scaleless, and it moved in a series of convulsive jerks through the profound silence of the sea's depth. Tembo forgot his fear and prepared to plunge from his position on the niggerhead.

He had pushed away from the outrigger and with his head once again under water, he glanced back at the bubble-sheathed hull of the canoe.

He was horrified to see Kamau struggling beside it. The bushbaby was paddling with hands and feet, but each time he kicked against the canoe's hull, he floated away from it. Already the weight of water in his fur was dragging him inexorably below the surface.

Tembo glanced from the bushbaby to the girl. She had turned to face her attacker, and seemed to be parrying it with her speargun. He turned back to Kamau whose struggles were getting visibly weaker.

The choice was an impossible one. If he tried to help the girl, Tembo would have to leave the bushbaby to drown. If he saved the bushbaby, he would sacrifice crucial seconds in which the girl could lose her battle.

She had plunged the speargun into the snapping jaws that seemed to be striking for her legs. She was a few feet below water, swimming on her back, her fingers still heroically fastened into the grouper's outspread gills.

Tembo launched himself awkwardly toward the canoe

and made a wild grab for the bushbaby. He was unprepared for the awful sensation of having no firm support beneath his feet. With his free hand he somehow discovered the canoe's gun'l and using this as a lever, he scooped Kamau out of the water and tossed the semiconscious bushbaby into the boat.

. When he turned back to Jackie, he saw that she had poked the speargun straight down her attacker's gullet. The jaws snapped tight on the wooden shaft. At once the rest of the body coiled like a spring. The girl heaved away the speargun and its loathsome victim and kicked frantically for the surface.

She was still gasping as she swam backstroke alongside Tembo.

"I hate those things," she said, coming to rest on the niggerhead. Seeing Tembo's expression, and interpreting this wrongly, she said: "It's all right. It was a moray eel. They don't often attack or bite like that." She spat. The salt water in her mouth reminded her of the eel.

Tembo said: "The bushbaby—"

She let go of the grouper. "What's happened?" The fish slapped the water with its tail and sank from sight, trailing the harpoon line.

"He's in the boat, baba. He fell in—"

She pulled one of the outrigger poles, and swung the canoe until she could scramble into it. The bushbaby lay sprawled in the bottom, eyes closed, in a pool of water.

She fell on hands and knees beside him. "Kamau!" Her voice was almost a shriek. She lifted the tiny body and saw water dribble from the half-closed mouth. He seemed lifeless.

The girl raised him to her lips. His fur had turned into stiff little spikes, revealing an alarmingly small body with a rat's tail. She pouted her lips and applied her mouth to his, blowing gently between the bared teeth. After thus breathing carefully into Kamau's mouth so that she inflated the waterlogged lungs, she pressed gently with hands cupped around his tiny chest and then listened to the gentle bubbling hiss of air that emerged. She did this several times, holding him nearly upside down.

Slowly he began to breathe again. A few seconds passed, and his eyelids fluttered.

"He lives," said Tembo.

The girl was shivering. Kamau was retching now, his body convulsed. She placed him on the hot planks of the canoe and ran worried fingers through his matted fur.

"How did this happen?"

Tembo was shocked by the fury in her eyes. "I don't know, baba."

"You must have rocked the canoe!" she accused him. She was shaking with rage.

Tembo clamped his mouth shut. He had seen mothers

react this way, after their babies had given them a bad fright.

"I should never have trusted you alone with him!" Jackie said, and she began to cry.

Then man moved slowly to the prow of the canoe and hauled in the stone-weighted rope. "We must go quickly," he said quietly. "Forget the fish."

The sun was already high. He began paddling back to the rivermouth, his face expressionless, eyes narrowed to slits as he watched for other fisherman. The girl lay sprawled in the bottom of the boat, still stroking the reviving bushbaby.

They moved into the river, the canoe shrouded in silence. Sometimes the girl glanced back at the man in the stern, paddling with a smooth steady rhythm. He avoided her eyes.

The river had lost its usual pace, denied the vital runoff of rainwater from the highlands. They had negotiated the tethered canoes safely, and now the water turned a chocolate brown full of little swirls and eddies.

Kamau stirred and sat up weakly. He blinked owlishly at the girl, and examined his arms and legs. He looked like a toothbrush, his fur still spikey, his tail bedraggled. He began cautiously to groom himself, combing the fur with the long currying nail on each of his little fingers. He chuckled as he did this, now and again glancing up at the girl.

She said, her face turned away from Tembo: "He seems fully recovered."

"I am glad," said the man.

"Perhaps I spoke too hastily," said the girl. "Forgive me."

"Of course, baba." But Tembo's voice was still non-committal.

"I lost my head," said the girl.

"It is understandable."

"I was very upset. It was no reason to be rude." Suddenly she turned and stretched out her hand, resting it lightly on the man's bared knee. "To rescue the bushbaby you must have had to swim?"

A great smile split his face from ear to ear, and around his eyes appeared a thousand small wrinkles of laughter. His teeth flashed in the sun and he said, choking: "Swim! Like a camel!"

She giggled. "Tembo, I'm truly sorry for what I said. Was it awful—*swimming?*"

She started to laugh too. Between them, the tension dissolved and left a new sense of comradeship. "It was terrible," he told her, and described the incident with many embellishments.

He stopped and his face became grave again. "It would be better if you put the galago on a lead now." He looked on either side at the slow-twisting banks of chocolate mud. Sometimes a river was drift-logged with crocodiles.

He felt no particular affection for Kamau but he also had a vision of Jackie's hysteria if the bushbaby vanished down a croc's gullet.

"You are right, old friend." Her voice was full of humility. She knew how quickly a seeming log was transformed into a racing crocodile, lifting itself like a battering ram on crooked legs, clear out of the mud and into the water without a ripple.

Kamau had finished his toilet. Experimentally, she handed him the last mint. He took it with such alacrity that she nursed no more doubts about his recovery. He held it between sticky fingers, curling his tongue lovingly around it, eyes rolling with ecstacy. Now was the time to slip his harness into place. She was appalled, however, by his appearance. The salt had dried in his fur. He was spiked like a porcupine.

"If only it would rain and wash him out," she thought. She searched the surrounding landscape. It was a patchwork of rural greens; bright yellow marked the young sugarcane; dark olive marked the bush; the farming shambas were a dancing green, and the exhausted banana fronds were dipped in a green of melancholy hue.

The land tilted like an easel. Soon it would be hard to navigate the river as it wound upward through the blue foothills that guarded the long approach to the Rift. Without rain, it was likely that the river would soon dry up altogether.

She began to untangle Kamau's lead.

The bushbaby paused in his otherwise engrossing task of licking the mint.

He twisted his head to one side, and the muscles in his legs stiffened.

Jackie unbuckled the small harness.

The bushbaby clucked his tongue softly, crouched on hands and knees, and scuttled away on all fours with the mint still enclosed in one hand. He paused at the feet of the man, and leaped flat onto the exposed knee.

Tembo was visibly shocked. The bushbaby had never shown him the slightest attention. Now he scuttled up the man's arm and squatted on his shoulder, once again sucking his mint.

Tembo stopped paddling and stared straight ahead, afraid to move his head.

"Baba," he whispered.

"What—?" Jackie looked up from her task. She was astonished to see the bushbaby abandon the mint and begin to lick Tembo's face.

The man sat stiff as a poker while the bushbaby explored his ear, pushing tiny fingers into the lobes.

"He's trying to thank you for saving his life," said the girl. "He's decided he likes you."

"He really likes me?"

"Of course."

"But I cannot paddle while he sits here."

"You can try."

The man reached carefully for his paddle. He got a curious sense of pleasure from this sudden display of friendship. For most Africans, the bushbaby was in every sense a jungle sprite, a creature with human-like characteristics that sometimes filled them with superstitious awe. Even Tembo shared this innate respect for bushbabies, knowing from observation that their family organization was quite complicated, and sensing their intelligence. His smile broadened.

The girl was overwhelmed with laughter at Tembo's mixed reaction of surprise and delight. She leaned backwards on her heels, supporting herself with hands pressed against the bare planks behind her.

"Paddle," she said.

"I dare not. Suppose he should fall again."

"He won't!" Her voice was emphatic. "You never need to teach Kamau a lesson twice. Isn't it strange how quickly he learns?" She became conversational, relishing the man's poker-backed immobility. "By the end of this journey, we shall have Kamau trained to run wild and free."

"You will miss him." The man spoke without turning his head, eyes swiveling to follow the bushbaby as it groped beyond his ear.

"Yes." She dropped her head and became busy again with the harness and lead. "It will be like losing a baby."

Meanwhile the canoe had been drifting toward the left bank. One of the outriggers caught in a trailing vine. Before the man could interfere, the canoe swung close against the twisting vegetation under wind-creaking palms. The canoe hit the bank and they were suddenly engulfed by a thick web of undergrowth.

Everything seemed to happen at once. The bushbaby hopped into the bottom of the boat where half a coconut husk floated in a few inches of water. A sunbird exploded from the bush, startling Tembo so that he dropped the paddle. While he fished for it and Jackie dived to rescue Kamau from his uneasy perch on the coconut shell, a thunderous roar burst upon them.

The noise was terrifying. It seemed like an endless roll of thunder, of rushing winds overlaid by a jet's high-pitched whine. The surface of the river boiled into chocolate eddies.

Jackie held the bushbaby with one hand and craned her head back. Between the gale-bent palm leaves she saw an Alouette jet helicopter.

It hung over them, only partly visible through the wind-divided branches. Then it tipped sideways and shot crabwise across the river. At once the wind fell and the canoe floated serenely under its forest camouflage.

They saw the helicopter creep along the opposite shore. A man in sky-blue dungarees stood on one of the helicopter skids, directing the pilot inside the perspex bubble.

The man on the skid had turned his binoculars downstream. The helicopter lifted its tail, spun round and whipped away. Almost at once the noise subsided, the river returned to its normal placid self, and the only sound was the cry of the white-bellied goaway bird. Its call was loud and rude: *"Go-away! Go-away! Go-away!"*

Cautiously, Jackie raised herself from the bottom of the canoe.

"They didn't see us." Her voice was triumphant. "They didn't see us."

She swooped on Kamau who had escaped again to curl up into a shivering bundle under one of the thwarts.

Tembo said shakily: "The galago saved us."

"Did you hear, Kamau?" The girl lifted the bushbaby into her lap. "If you hadn't played games with Tembo, we would have been out in the middle of the river."

The man resumed his seat in the stern and dipped his paddle again in the water. "Twice this morning we have been saved from discovery." He thrust the canoe out from the overgrown bank. "It is a lucky sign."

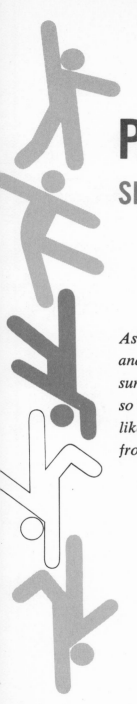

Pulga

SINY ROSE VAN ITERSON

*As the squalor of inner-city Bogotá
and roadside banditry change to the
surrounding beauty of the mountains,
so the life of a fourteen-year-old boy
like Pulga ("the flea") can shift overnight
from misery and danger to hope.*

Gilimon Naranjo

There was no sign of a letup in the rainy season. Dark clouds came from the llanos over the mountains and dropped torrents of rain over the city. Hailstones bounced off the streets, piled high along the sidewalks, clogged the sewers. The streets were a mesh of dirty rivers. From the bare hills, heavy, yellowish mud, which looked like lava, oozed down. Gravel and stones were carried along into the streets of the city, stalling traffic.

Pulga stood in the doorway of the room where he lived, up to his ankles in the water. He kept staring at the rain. The hail and rubbish from the broken gutter had clogged up the drain. The patio was a vast lake, and water was running into the rooms.

Pulga's grandmother sat huddled on the bed. His two little sisters had snuggled up against her. The water in the room was five inches deep.

Pedro came along with an old broom. "I got it from Joaquin," he said, and began sweeping.

Pulga watched him for a while, then said, "It's no good. The drain is clogged. The water comes back in as fast as you sweep it out. Can't you see?" . . .

Nothing could be done. The rain kept falling out of the gray sky in buckets.

"Ave María, Virgen Santa," mumbled the old grand-mother on her bed. The little girls, numb with cold, snuggled up to her still closer. Pulga pulled his head down between his shoulders, and with a few bold jumps he got across the patio to the paved passageway. Soaked to the skin, he stood by the main door looking up and down the street. . . .

His mother had died after the birth of his youngest sister, and then his father had stopped coming home altogether. Consuelo, his oldest sister, had found a job in another part of town. She paid the rent, and occasionally she brought something to eat or a piece of worn-out clothing. His grandmother, who had been living with them for some time, stayed on. . . .

When the rain let up, Pulga went to the marketplace in the center of town, where he usually spent much of his time trying to earn a few pennies as a car watcher.

In this weather few cars were there to be watched. The market was a sad sight with its soaked bags, baskets, produce, and muddy paths between the stands. Women sat crouching beside their wares, water dripping from the brims of their men's hats.

Pulga ran up to a car that was about to park. "Let me watch, let me watch!" he shouted. . . .

A man shoved him aside. . . .

"Get going, boy," the man ordered, when Pulga tried to resist. . . .

Pulga moved on.

. . . He tightened the string holding up the trousers that were much too big for him and walked on aimlessly, up one street, down another.

To go home where everything was underwater and where his grandmother and his sisters were crouching on the bed made no sense. There might be barely enough room for Pedro, but not for the five of them.

He kept going until he came to a street full of big trucks. The place was busy, with drivers, *ruanas* over their shoulders, walking around the vehicles, checking waybills, freight, the trucks themselves. They shouted, laughed, swore, slapped each other on the shoulder, and wandered in groups or singly back and forth between the coffee shops and their jobs.

The unceasing din of honking horns was deafening. As soon as one truck left the lineup and drove away, another arrived to fill its place. The heavy trucks were dusty and spattered, their wheels covered with mud. They had traveled thousands of miles, over poor roads, across the mountains, through the sweltering heat of the flatlands, along precipitous cliffs, through the mist and across the treeless plateaus called *páramos*.

Pulga stopped to look at one of the huge trucks. The trailer was supported by axles with enormous double wheels. He counted them one by one. There were eight of them. The red cab was shining, the headlights and the chrome bumpers were shining. The large mirrors outside the side windows were shining too. Written over the windshield were the words *Mi Amor*. The motor hummed softly. The driver was standing on the front bumper, the upper half of his body hidden under the open hood.

Pulga sneaked up to the cab. He could feel the warmth of the motor. Heavy drops were tapping again on the pavement; once more it began to pour. Within a few moments the street was deserted. The men had fled into the coffee shops. The driver, who had been standing on the bumper of his truck, closed the hood, stopped the motor, and ran to join the others.

Pulga looked around. Except for the coffee shops, where they would have chased him out anyway, there was no shelter in sight. Without a second thought, he slipped under the truck and sat down between the rear wheels. He heard the rain drumming on the canvas roof high above his head. But it did not bother him now. Where he was sitting, it was nice and dry. He stretched out, rested his chin on his hands, and looked at the raindrops, glittering in the light from the shops. His eyelids were as heavy as lead. His head sank down. Pulga was asleep.

Inside the coffee shop, Gilimon Naranjo said to his friends, "That takes care of the grease job. Tomorrow morning I'll be off again." He paid his bill and, pulling his head down between his shoulders, ran across the street to his truck.

The driver jumped into his cab, started the motor, opened the side window, and wiped the fogged windshield. Shifting into gear, he stepped slowly on the gas pedal. The wheels began to turn.

Outside, through the downpour, a voice called out, "Gilimon, hold it! Someone's underneath!"

Gilimon turned the steering wheel.

"Gilimon!"

Gilimon stuck his head out the side window. "What's wrong?"

"There's someone underneath!"

With a curse, Gilimon jumped out of the cab.

The man who had called out to him was staring under the body of the truck at the back, his hands on his knees. Several men in the coffee shop came out leaving their drinks behind.

Gilimon bent down and dragged Pulga out from between the wheels. "What the devil . . . you brat!" he shouted.

Pulga, still half asleep, stared into Gilimon's face. Slowly he stood up and looked around to make his getaway, but Gilimon had a tight grip on his arm.

"That was a narrow escape," said the man who had warned Gilimon. With obvious satisfaction he went on his way while the others went back to their drinks.

Gilimon and Pulga faced each other in the pouring rain. "OK," said Gilimon, "what the devil did you think you were doing?"

Pulga said nothing.

"Well. . . ." said Gilimon.

"I . . . I didn't do anything," stammered Pulga. "I was asleep. I must have been asleep."

"Asleep, under my truck! What have you got a head for? Just think, those wheels of mine were ready to crush you to a pulp. Why don't you go home to sleep?"

Pulga shrugged. "At home everything is underwater," he said flatly. "My grandmother and my sisters are sitting on the bed. . . . Pedro and I always sleep on the floor, but with this rain and all. . . ."

Gilimon looked at the drenched boy standing in front of him. "Come on," he said, "we can't stay here," and led Pulga into the coffee shop.

"Hungry?" Gilimon asked. He did not wait for an answer and ordered a bowl of soup. When it arrived, along with potatoes and yucca, he said, "Where do you live?"

"Over there, up the hill," answered Pulga between spoonfuls.

"With your grandmother?"

Pulga nodded and went on eating.

"What about your parents? No parents?"

Pulga shook his head.

"What's your name?"

"Pulga."

"What do you do for food?"

No answer.

"Just hanging around in the streets all day long?"

"I watch cars in the marketplace. But today a man was there in a black coat. He chased me away."

"So you are out of work now," Gilimon observed with a smile.

Pulga nodded. His bowl was empty. With a sigh he put down the spoon.

"Want another?"

Pulga nodded.

Gilimon motioned to the waiter, then said slowly, "Well, I need a boy for my truck. I had a helper but he left me in the lurch, just when I must be off again. But I guess you're too young. . . ."

"I'm fifteen," Pulga said quickly.

Gilimon looked at the boy. He couldn't expect to get much out of such a skinny, undersized beanstalk. No strength in those matchstick arms. But then, it was a toss-up. He thought of the helper on his last trip. The fellow was strong as an ox, and bright too, but as lazy as they come. It was no credit to him that the entire load had not been stolen from the truck while he was sitting in the cab, taking it easy. And when he, Gilimon, had told him what he thought of him, the young gentleman took offense and quit.

Pulga was gulping down his second bowl of soup.

Gilimon said, "I'll take you along."

"What!" Pulga's spoon stopped halfway to his mouth.

"You can come along on the truck tomorrow," Gilimon said. "You'll have to tell your people that I don't know for certain when I'm going to be back. Before Christmas, I hope. It depends on the kind of hauling jobs they give me. Whatever it is, that's it. Tomorrow I'll drive over to Cúcuta."

He got up. In his shiny leather jacket he towered above Pulga. "Want to come along?" he asked.

Pulga just nodded.

"Then I'll see you in the morning. My truck will be standing two blocks down the street at the gas station on the corner. Don't forget to tell your people that I don't know when I'll be back. And make sure you're on time. I have to leave at half past three."

Pulga was so flabbergasted that he did not notice that his soup bowl, with a whole potato still in it, had been taken away. In a daze he went outside. Gilimon's huge truck was rolling down the street, disappearing around the corner.

Pulga ran all the way to the gas station, but Gilimon was gone. The truck, however, was there in all its glory.

Deciding to be on the safe side, he did not bother to go home at all. Quick as a cat he climbed up on the truck and hid under the heavy canvas. Tomorrow morning at half past three he was going to be there. On the dot! Except for Pedro, no one in the big house would miss him.

Mama Maruja's Place
Bogotá to Cúcuta

The rain came pouring down again as they drove out of the city.

Pulga sat bolt upright in the cab, staring through the large windshield. Never before had he been inside an automobile. Never before had he seen the city in this way. Dark rows of houses were gliding past him. The Avenida Caracas came zooming into the headlights. A man was walking across the road. A car came whizzing past them. A night watchman was standing in a doorway.

The rain kept beating against the windshield, but inside the cab it was dry. The windshield wipers swept across the line of sight, left-right, right-left. . . . Gradually the lights from the housing development that stretched far out into the savanna dropped back into nothingness. They had left the city behind.

The countryside was dark, the air gray. The high ragged mountains, the eastern chains of the Andes, merged with the lead-colored masses of clouds. The big truck rolled along the road; the motor hummed monotonously. Gilimon kept looking straight ahead, his hairy fists clenched over the steering wheel.

Pulga stealthily peered up at him.

"How are you doing?" asked Gilimon without taking his eyes off the road.

"Fine," Pulga whispered, still so taken aback by everything that he could hardly speak. His fingers fidgeted along the edges of the suitcase standing between his legs. It was Gilimon's suitcase.

Slowly, very slowly, the darkness in the valleys receded. The green hilltops were the first to be hit by the rays of the rising sun. Eucalyptus trees and weeping willows along the shoulders of the road began to take shape in the morning mist. The savanna spread out before them. The mountains stood out sharply against the lighted sky.

They drove through small villages. People appeared on the road. They came out of the hills, from remote settlements, from scattered hovels in the valleys to take their produce to the town market. A bagful of potatoes or yucca, a basket of Indian corn, a string of onions. The men rode on sturdy little horses; the baskets and bags were carried by mules and women.

Outside of Tunja they stopped for a quick bowl of soup with chunks of meat, potatoes, and onions, and a cup of hot chocolate. . . .

In a cloud of stinking black smoke the truck started up and got back onto the road. . . .

Pulga sat straight up in the cab and looked out into this new world, a new green world, which he had not known existed. "What is that place again we're going to?" he asked.

"Cúcuta, didn't I tell you?"

"Oh, yes," Pulga said quickly. After a while he cautiously ventured another question. "Is it far?"

"Yes and no. It all depends on what you mean by far," said Gilimon casually. "It's over by the Venezuelan border."

Pulga had nothing more to ask. The word Cúcuta meant nothing to him and the word Venezuelan even less. But what did it matter? Here he was, sitting in this marvelous giant of a truck, far away from that filthy wet hole in the big dark house in midtown. For the first time in his life he was not hungry. And he had a job! Who would have thought of such a thing? Pulga sat up still straighter. He breathed deeply and raised his head higher. For a moment he thought of Pedro. What was Pedro doing now?

But then his eyes caught sight again of the sunny countryside that kept speeding by as he looked out the windows. His attention was absorbed by a thousand new and strange things: the cows in the pastures, the waving treetops, the play of light and shadow on the slopes of the mountains. He was not thinking of Pedro anymore.

Gilimon slowed down and turned into a small country road. They followed its winding course through the hills and came to a little sun-bathed valley surrounded by silvery eucalyptus trees. A little brook wound through the green pasture land. Higher up were dark fir trees, and from the rocks fell a stream of water. The hum of the little waterfall filled the peaceful valley. Gilimon stopped outside a barbed-wire fence. On the other side a narrow path led along a field of Indian corn to a small house.

"Is this it?' asked Pulga.

"It? What do you mean? Oh, you think we're in Cúcuta. Think again, if you can. Cúcuta is still a long way off. This is where Mamá Maruja lives. Mamá Maruja is my godmother. I always drop in here whenever I happen to be in the neighborhood. Step on it, Pulga, open the gate. I didn't bring you along just for the ride."

Pulga jumped out as fast as he could and ran up to the fence. Gilimon watched him desperately trying to get the better of the rickety gate that seemed to be resisting him. Finally it was open. Gilimon wondered once again whether he had done the right thing in taking on such a skinny shrimp for his trip. That flea, he feared, was going to be more trouble than he was worth. With a sigh he drove through the gate, up the bumpy dirt road leading to Mamá Maruja's house. Pulga came running behind the truck. A couple of angry barking dogs dashed out from the house, and Pulga clambered up the truck like a scared cat. At that moment a woman in a black dress came out of the house. She was thin and angular, with a parched, wrinkled face and strong muscular arms.

When she saw Gilimon, her face lit up. Her dark piercing eyes sparkled, and the network of wrinkles in her taut face relaxed.

"Blessed be the day!" she called out. "This gladdens my heart."

She put her arms around Gilimon and patted his back over and over. "What's new? What do you have to say for yourself?" she asked.

Then her eyes fell on Pulga. "For the love of God," she exclaimed with surprise. "What have you got there?" She tucked a strand of shining black hair back under her man's hat and looked searchingly at Pulga.

"That is my new helper," said Gilimon and laughed. "He is afraid he might be eaten alive."

Mamá Maruja chased the dogs away. "Now you can come down," she said to Pulga.

"Did you bring my suitcase?" asked Gilimon. "Remember it at all times. You must never leave it behind in the cab. I have my money and all my clothes in it."

"And his shaving mirror with the picture of his girl friend stuck to the back," added Mamá Maruja. "And never the same one twice." She shook her head. "I just wonder when you'll get serious, Gilimon. It's time for you to settle down."

Still shaking her head, she led the way to the other side of the house. Gilimon sat down on the wooden bench that was there and stretched out his legs, evidently feeling quite at home. Mamá Maruja picked up the altar cloth that she had been mending and sat down next to him. Chickens were scratching in the dust, pigs and the two dogs were lying outside the door to the smoke-blackened kitchen, and a bleating goat was tugging at its tether. Pulga felt rather strange with all these animals around and kept looking uncertainly at the dogs.

Meanwhile, Mamá Maruja had gotten up again and disappeared into the small kitchen. A moment later she came back with a large bowl of black coffee for Gilimon. She turned to Pulga. "Here, this is for you," she said, and handed him a gourd shell filled with goat's milk. She watched him as he drank greedily.

"Poor child," she said pityingly. "Skin and bones. How did you get hold of him?"

"It just worked out that way," answered Gilimon. "My helper ran away yesterday. Then I found him. I don't expect to get much out of him, but I suppose he's better than no helper at all."

Mamá Maruja turned to Pulga. "What is your name?" she asked.

"Pulga."

"What did you say?"

"Pulga."

"Pulga? Flea? That cannot be your real name, can it?"

Pulga did not answer. Embarrassed, he dug his bare feet into the dust.

"Tell me now, what is your name, your real name?"

Pulga remained silent. He could not understand why Mamá Maruja should want to know his name. No one ever had asked him that question. He almost had forgotten his name himself. Finally he mumbled in a low voice, "Francisco José."

"Francisco José," Mamá Maruja repeated. "That is what I call a nice name. Not like Pulga. Pulga is not right. From now on I will call you Francisco José."

Then she turned again to Gilimon. "And now," she said, "let's hear the news. Are you coming down from Cúcuta?"

"No, I'm on my way there."

"So you still have quite a trip ahead of you."

"That's for certain. We started out this morning at half past three."

"I see," said Mamá Maruja. "I'm going to make soup for you. After that you will feel fit again." She went back into her kitchen.

"But I can't stay long," objected Gilimon. "I want to get past the stretch where García Rovira is before dark."

Mamá Maruja looked out the kitchen door and nodded. "The Rovira crowd are bad," she said. "Robbers, that's what they are. They fight each other and kill at the drop of a hat. When it isn't politics, it's personal. That's the way it is. Francisco José, go and find me some kindling wood, and then carry in some more water, and go and pick a few ears of corn, but nice ones, young and juicy, you hear? I must make some soup for you, Gilimon. You like my *mazamorra*, don't you? After all, the boy has got to eat something."

Gilimon stopped objecting. No one could argue with Mamá Maruja. She would agree with everything, and then proceed as she wanted to in the first place.

Pulga was busy gathering wood and carrying water and picking corn.

Mamá Maruja looked pleased. "That's the kind of boy I ought to have," she said. "I'm not getting younger, Gilimon. . . . There are the sheep that must be watched, the pigs and the goat to be taken care of. Water must be brought in from the brook each day. Firewood must be gathered. The corn must be harvested. And before you know it, it's time again to plant potatoes. . . ." She sighed. "A boy like you would come in handy," she repeated, as Pulga passed by with an armful of kindling.

She disappeared again into her little smoke-blackened

kitchen. Gilimon folded his hands over his stomach and closed his eyes.

Pulga looked uncertainly toward the dogs, and then walked off in the direction of the brook, where he had gone to get water. Along the edge of it, on huge boulders, Mamá Maruja's wash was spread out to bleach. Sunlight flickered over the running water and cast delicate designs of bright and dark spots on the ground under the trees. From behind the eucalyptus trees came the steady hum of the waterfall. Pulga walked a short distance and then he jumped to a large, flat boulder halfway across the brook. The clear icy water washed his dirty feet and thin ankles. The sun was burning on his back, the air was warm and soft. Slowly Pulga waded upstream. The water felt like a soothing balm. Near the rocks, where the foaming waterfall came down, Pulga stopped and looked at the spray of droplets that glistened and glittered in a thousand colors under the sunlight.

On a sudden impulse, he took off his stinking rags and flung them on the ground along the edge of the brook. Stark-naked he walked to the waterfall and stood under it. He let the water splash down on him, over his shoulders and his back. He stretched out his arms. Then he bent down, scooped up a handful of fine sand from under the pebbles and began to scour his body. The water streamed down over him. His skin prickled, and his blood began to tingle. He was alive, and his name was Francisco José!

Finally he stepped out from under the falling water and carefully looked over his arms, his legs, his body. He was almost clean. When he saw his dirty clothes, he hesitated for a moment. Then, crouching on his haunches, he began as best he could to scrub his shirt and his pants. He spread them out to dry on the stones, just the way Mamá Maruja's wash was spread out.

With his arms wrapped around his knees, he sat for a while staring at the flecks of foam that drifted past him on the water. They looked like little white flowers, airily dancing along with the whirling currents. He did not know how long he had been sitting there when suddenly he realized that he was being called.

"Francisco José! Francisco José!"

Hastily he slipped on his damp clothes and ran back.

Gilimon already had sat down to eat, and a bowl of steaming soup stood ready for Pulga. He looked sideways at Mamá Maruja, feeling uncertain, almost distrustful. She had called him to come and eat. He could hardly believe it. Hastily he gulped down the big bowl of soup. With a sigh of satisfaction, he put the spoon down and looked gratefully at Mamá Maruja.

When they drove off, she stood at the gate. A woman with a hard and inscrutable face, her strong arms folded over her chest, her back straight. A woman like many others in the mountain country of Colombia, unswerving, God-fearing, and unbendable.

"*Que la* Santa Virgen *les acompañe*," she called out after them. "May the Virgin Mary be with you."

To the Páramo del Almorzadero

The road climbed for a long time, then began to slope down again. They drove into the valley of the Chicamocha River. The mountains stretched out endlessly, bare, hard, deserted. Pastel-colored peaks dissolved in the hazy distance. Far below them flowed the Chicamocha River, its banks green, its bed eroded. High and unreachable rose the steep and somber mountain slopes. The highest peaks were hidden in the clouds.

The farther they went the warmer it became. Rattling buses, with misfiring engines and machine-gunning exhausts, their drivers leaning on their horns, dashed past them. Hot dust blew into the cab. The road gravel was picked up by the tires and hurled down over the edge into the valley below.

Sugarcane and tobacco grew on the hillsides, white cattle stood dully at the riverbanks. In the valleys it was burning hot. The trees and bushes were gray with dust;

no breeze stirred the date palms. They drove across the bridge over the Chicamocha River and through Capitanejo, the small village on the other side.

Then the road began to climb again. The motor strained, working hard. Once more they were driving into the mountains. The sun lost its force. The light grew dimmer and shadows settled down between the hills. Though it was dark around the trees and bushes, the air was a blaze of red and yellow and orange, a fierce air that did not give off light but instead drained all color from the earth.

Gilimon looked at his watch. "We should not have stayed at Mamá Maruja's as long as we did," he said.

"I thought it was nice," said Pulga from the depths of his heart.

Gilimon looked at him sideways. "You did, did you?" he said. Then, with a teasing little laugh, he added, "What were you up to there? You lost half your tan."

Pulga stared out the window. "I went to the waterfall. I washed up," he mumbled. "All the way under the water. I stood right under it. It was nice."

"Cold, I guess?" said Gilimon.

"Well, no . . . yes, it was cold. But it wasn't bad. The sun was nice and warm. . . ."

"We should not have stayed as long as we did," Gilimon said again. "I don't drive along this stretch in the dark. Too many holdups. The people around here are no good. They work hard, but you can't trust them, and they don't give a damn. They'll shoot you down for no reason, like a bird in the field. And don't imagine that the police will ever do anything about it. They just shrug and raise their arms over their heads."

Gilimon shifted gears. Slowly the truck pulled up the steep and lonely road. "And among themselves," he went on, "they're no better. They think they can settle their accounts by themselves, without the help of the police. An eye for an eye, a tooth for a tooth, that's their way. A nice bunch!"

It was getting unpleasantly cold. Now the mountains were bare of trees. Only frailejóns with long woolly leaves, like donkeys' ears, grew on the slopes between barren dark underbrush. Fog rolled over the mountaintops, settled in the valleys, rose up between the high bushes, and swept in patches over the road.

The headlights picked up eerie formations, sweeping ahead of the moving truck. Figures of women in white gauze, luring them on along the narrow road, higher into the darkness, into the cold, into nothingness. . . .

"Damn it all, there we have it!" Gilimon slammed on the brakes so hard that Pulga banged his head into the windshield. With a jolt, the truck came to a stop. The road was blocked with heavy boulders.

From behind the frailejóns along the roadside three men appeared out of the fog. Handkerchiefs covered their faces, and only their eyes were visible under the rims of their sweat-soaked felt hats. In one leap they were at the door of the cab.

"Get out and keep quiet," said the leader without raising his voice.

Gilimon turned to Pulga, but the seat was empty. The door on the other side stood open. Pulga was gone.

Gilimon slowly stepped down, trying to keep his back covered by the truck. The three men surrounded him.

"Where is your helper?"

"Who?"

"Don't try to be funny. Where is your helper, your assistant, whatever you call him? You're not alone."

"The door on this side is open, Chief," called out one of the highwaymen who had walked around the truck. "Didn't I tell you? He's gone."

"*Caramba*, don't stand there watching the moon!" the chief shouted. "Go and look for him! And be quick about it. I'll watch this one." Then, turning to Gilimon, he said, "Take one false step, and I'll let you have it full in the face! Where's your money?" Expertly he began to search Gilimon.

The two others ran around the truck, looked under it, inside it, among the frailejóns, in the ditch along the shoulder of the road, in the shadows of fallen rocks.

"Got him?" asked the leader impatiently.

"He isn't anywhere," answered the men.

"You're useless! He must be around. He couldn't have gone far. Be sure you get him. I don't want him sneaking up on us from behind. . . ."

From the mountains came a rumbling noise, loud blasts, and the honking of a horn. Yellow spots of light appeared, were gone again, then reappeared around one of the bends in the road.

The leader cursed and swore. "See that? Someone coming along from the Páramo," he said furiously. "Take that stuff off the truck and be quick about it. This fellow has no money on him. Find his bag in the cab. Hurry, there isn't much time left. . . ."

In the rear of the truck the canvas was ripped open, crates and baskets were pulled out and dropped on the ground. Gilimon was knocked out by a blow on his chin. By the time the bus from Cúcuta reached the barricade, the bandits had disappeared.

Now the deserted mountain road suddenly came to life. Passengers carrying bundles, boxes, bags, baskets came tumbling out of the bus. Women dragged children and carried chickens. One man had a live pig under his arm; another clutched an *aguardiente* bottle.

"What happened?"

"The road is blocked."

"A raid, a highway job! They knocked out the driver!"

"A raid! Ave María Purísima!"

They poured some *aguardiente* into Gilimon and

helped him to his feet. They offered him another mouthful of *aguardiente* and drowned him in a flood of questions.

Meanwhile, a few of the men had begun to clear the road. The bus driver walked slowly around the truck and surveyed the damage. "They've taken some of your load, and your canvas is torn," he reported to Gilimon.

"How did it happen?" asked someone.

"How many were there?"

Suddenly Gilimon saw Pulga standing in the middle of the crowd. "Where did you come from?" he asked.

"I . . . I just sat there," answered Pulga, his voice slightly hoarse.

"Where? Where were you sitting?"

"There . . . under the truck."

"Under the truck? Impossible! They looked under the truck!"

"I did sit there. . . ."

Gilimon looked at him in disbelief. Then he caught sight of something Pulga held clutched against his body. "What have you got there? Is that my suitcase?" he asked unnecessarily.

Pulga nodded.

"You have to report this robbery in Pamplona," advised the bus driver. "Otherwise they may think that you made away with the stuff yourself. Those fellows are gone for good. They'll never get caught."

Gilimon nodded vaguely. "Yes, yes . . ." he said, still unable to think clearly. "I'm going to report it right away. Right away . . . in Pamplona."

"A lucky thing for you that we happened to come along," the bus driver said. "Otherwise they might have gotten away with the whole load. They might have done away with you, too—kkrrsh." To make quite clear what he meant he moved his hand swiftly across his throat. "We should have been past here long before this. I don't like to be on this part of the road after dark, but we had trouble up on the Páramo. Well, I don't have to tell you anything, I guess."

The passengers, with their assorted treasures, climbed back into the bus. The children, the chickens, the pig, the cardboard boxes, the filled baskets, and the bulky bags were stowed away, for better or worse, in the aisle. The driver sat down behind the wheel; his helper jumped up on the running board.

"Good-bye now."

"Good-bye and many thanks."

"Not at all."

"Good luck. . . ."

The bus started moving. Honking its horn it rolled downhill.

Gilimon and Pulga drove on into the mountains, up and up to the Páramo del Almorzadero. It was dark and bitter cold, and the wind was pitiless. Pulga sat huddled up in the corner of the cab.

"Seriously now, tell me where you were hiding," said Gilimon.

"Under the truck."

"Those fellows looked everywhere," Gilimon said slowly. "All along the road and up behind the frailejóns. They looked under the truck, too. . . ."

"I was sitting up on the axle."

"On the what?"

"On the axle between the wheels."

"With my suitcase?"

"Yes."

"On the axle between the wheels with a suitcase." Gilimon was completely dumbfounded. "First I have to pull him out from under my truck where he's asleep between the wheels, and then he climbs up on the axle. What do you suppose would have happened if the truck had moved, you ass! Don't you understand that you would have been crushed to a pulp? What were you thinking of? Tell me!"

"I was not thinking at all," admitted Pulga sheepishly. "I was afraid . . . and . . . and you told me that I must look out for the suitcase. You said that I should never leave it behind in the truck."

Gilimon said nothing further. He looked once or twice

out of the corner of his eye at the benumbed little boy sitting there next to him. His helper. After a while he mumbled more to himself than to Pulga, "We can thank our stars that the bus from Cúcuta came along. Otherwise not much would be left, that's for certain. The way it was, we got away by the skin of our teeth. In Pamplona I'll have to report the whole thing to the police."

"I thought you said that the police would do nothing," said Pulga. He was not very eager to have anything to do with the police. Policemen had never been particularly friendly to him, and his love for them was lukewarm at best.

"What I said was that they would never find out who held us up. But I have to report such things the first chance I get. In this case, that means Pamplona. Just to keep things straight, you know. Otherwise I have to pay for the damage out of my own pocket. What's the matter? Are you cold?"

Pulga nodded, his teeth chattering.

"There's an old *ruana* under the seat. Take it—you can have it."

The truck hummed along across the bare deserted tableland, over the roof of the world, across the Páramo del Almorzadero. The headlights swept over the hard frozen ground. No trees, no bushes, nothing seemed to be growing.

Once in a while the dark cold expanse of a landlocked

lake appeared. Sometimes the yellow light caught huge, eerie boulders ground smooth by driving winds, faded and shaped by endless rains. Like mighty monsters turned into stone, they rose up from the darkness and fell back again into their world of shadows.

The wind howled around the truck. Cold and smooth as metal, the sky hung suspended over the black countryside. There was no trace of life anywhere, no hut, no animal, no light. Dark and lonely and ice-cold. Pulga sat huddled up in his *ruana*. His head dropped down on his chest.

So they drove on to Pamplona.

Sumi and the Goat and the Tokyo Express

YOSHIKO UCHIDA

Sumi lives in a tiny, quiet village in Japan,
far away from big city excitement.
Therefore, when her next-door neighbor,
very old Mr. Oda, gets a new goat,
Sumi senses adventures in the air.

umi flung off her shoes at the entrance and burst into the house.

"Mama!" she shouted. "Guess what has come to Mr. Oda's house."

Mr. Oda was their ninety-nine-year-old neighbor and one of Sumi's best friends. She had just stopped to see him on the way home from school and was going to hurry back as soon as she found a proper present for the new arrival.

Mother was in the kitchen washing the rice for supper, and Sumi followed the sounds to find her. There was a nice busy sound and an easy rhythm to the way Mother's hand swung around and around in the pan. She scarcely looked up as Sumi called, and her hand kept right on swishing the rice. Sumi came home so often with all sorts of news that nothing much could startle her.

"What is it, Sumi Chan?" she asked. "Did Mr. Oda get a new fence post for his front gate?"

"No, something much better," Sumi declared.

"A new stone for his garden?"

"No, no! It's alive! It's something alive!"

"Ah," Mother said. And then, because she knew that Sumi couldn't wait to tell, she said, "I cannot guess. You must tell me." And she put the rice aside so it could rest until it was time to be cooked.

"He got a new goat and she will give him fresh milk every day," Sumi explained quickly. "She came on a truck from Kasa Village and her name is Miki."

"Mah," Mother said, looking pleased. "How nice for Mr. Oda."

"I'm going to take her a 'welcome-to-Sugi-Village' present," Sumi said, and she hurried to her room to see what she could find.

What would be a suitable gift for a pet goat? Maybe she would like some caramels, Sumi thought, or a bag of rice crackers. But Sumi wanted to give her something that would last. She looked in all her drawers and finally found an old red hat that Mother had knit for her one winter. It had a hole on the side, but Sumi pinched it together with a safety pin and hoped no one would notice. It would be a fine gift, especially with the cold winds of winter coming soon.

When Sumi returned to Mr. Oda's house, she found him hobbling about his yard, leaning on his old gnarled cane and wearing his big black cape to keep out the chill. His cheeks were puffed with two sour lemon balls, one on each side, and he walked slowly around his new pet, admiring her from all sides. His pet peacock, Saburo, strutted behind him, making strange sounds in his throat and darting quick, suspicious glances at the strange new creature that had come to share his yard.

Behind them all hovered the old housekeeper, fluttering her big white apron and trying to chase Saburo away.

"Shoo!" she shouted at him. "Shoo, shoo!" But Saburo didn't pay the slightest attention to her.

"I brought a present for Miki," Sumi called, waving her red hat in the air. "It's to keep her head warm."

She edged up to the white goat tethered to the plum tree and wrinkled her nose. Miki might be a fine goat, but she certainly didn't smell very nice. Sumi and Miki looked at each other and Sumi reached out to put her hat on Miki's head.

"There," she said, backing away quickly. She wasn't at all sure that she liked Mr. Oda's new pet.

The old man, however, was very pleased with everyone. He clapped his thin hands together and laughed happily.

"That is a marvelous gift," he exclaimed. "Now Miki looks like a goat with some character." And he reached inside his *kimono* sleeve and found two sour lemon balls for Sumi.

The housekeeper looked at Miki wearing her new hat and laughed until the tears rolled down her cheeks. *"Mah, mah,"* she sputtered, "I have seen a good many things in my long life, but I have never seen a goat wearing a hat." And she held her sides and laughed some more. "I'll cut some holes for her ears," she said, "so the hat won't fall off."

"Now come inside, little one," the old man said, reaching a hand toward Sumi. "Miki has a present for you too."

It was a glass of fresh goat's milk, and it was still warm. Sumi liked milk, but she had never tasted goat's milk before. She held her breath and took a big gulp.

"Ugh!" she said before she could stop herself. She couldn't drink another drop, even if it *had* come from a goat with character. It would be something new to tell the class the next day, however, and Sumi could hardly wait to be the first one to speak.

Every morning at ten o'clock, Sumi's second-grade class put away their books and anyone who had some special news would stand up to tell the class about it. Sometimes their teacher, who was also the mayor of Sugi Village, would tell about something he had read in the newspapers. Sometimes he told them about Tokyo or Osaka, but at other times he would tell about such far away places as America or Africa or China.

Mr. Mayor, of course, usually had the most interesting things to tell. But after him, it was Ayako, who sat in front of Sumi. Her father owned the village rice shop, and he knew everything about everyone in the village. One day Sumi wanted to tell some news that not even Ayako knew about.

Maybe today is that day, Sumi thought, as she went to school the next morning. She raised her hand the moment Mr. Mayor asked if anyone had some news, and she stood up before Ayako had a chance to speak.

"I had a drink of fresh milk yesterday," she said proudly, "straight from a brand new goat who just came to our village. The goat is Mr. Oda's new pet," Sumi went on. "She came from Kasa Village in a truck and I gave her a red hat for a present."

All the children laughed at the thought of a goat wearing a red hat.

"Well," Mr. Mayor began.

But already Ayako's hand was fluttering in the air. She stood up and spoke in a loud, clear voice, and her news was so exciting that everyone immediately forgot all about Mr. Oda's goat. She told that a railroad was going to be built along the edge of their village only one hundred yards away from the school. It would be the first railroad that ever came so close to Sugi Village.

"It's going to come through the mountains and come out right over there," Ayako said. And she pointed toward the windows that looked out over the rice fields. Everyone listened carefully, because if Ayako said so, it must be true.

Sumi sighed and slumped back in her chair. If only Miki had been something more exciting than an old, white goat. If only she had been a kangaroo or a chimpanzee or an elephant. But what was a mere goat compared to a whole railroad? Nothing, Sumi thought dismally, nothing at all.

Sumi had never ridden on a train, nor had most of her classmates. After all, none of them had ever needed or wanted to leave Sugi Village. There was a great clamor in the classroom as everyone began to talk at once.

"Yes, yes. It is quite true," Mr. Mayor said. "A railroad is indeed coming, and the train will be an express straight from Tokyo."

Now even Sumi forgot about Mr. Oda's goat. A Tokyo Express travelling so close to the village was something wonderful to think about. Ayako's news *was* more exciting. There was no doubt about that.

As soon as she got home, Sumi told her mother about the railroad; and at suppertime she told Father and her big brother, Taro.

Father did not sound very excited or happy to hear the news. "So it is coming at last," he said in a quiet voice, for he was thinking of the rice fields that would be plowed under to make way for the railroad.

Sumi thought Mother looked a little sad too. Only Taro, who was ten and thought he knew more about everything than Sumi, seemed excited.

"If we get a railroad, maybe we'll have a station someday," he said. "And if we get a station, maybe the Tokyo Express will stop here!"

"Will it?" Sumi wondered.

No one knew. "I'll ask tomorrow," she said.

As soon as Sumi got to school the next day, she asked

Mr. Mayor if the express would ever stop at their village.

Mr. Mayor shook his head. "No, it is a high-speed express and it will stop only at a few large cities," he explained.

"It will never stop here then?" Sumi asked.

"I'm afraid not," Mr. Mayor answered, and even his round, cheerful face looked somber.

"It will never, never stop in Sugi Village," Ayako announced firmly. "My father said so." And, of course, Ayako's father knew everything.

Now the long wait for the express began. Soon the rice was harvested and the fields were prepared for the planting of winter wheat. The maple leaves turned red and gold and then drifted from the trees to the ground. The persimmon grew orange and ripe for eating and there were chestnuts to roast in the warm charcoal embers. The sky grew brilliant and clear, and at day's end the stars seemed frozen in the darkness of winter nights.

Soon a tunnel was bored through the mountain and the tracks were laid across what was once a rice field at the eastern edge of the village. Every day Taro and his friends went to watch the work on the railroad, and sometimes they let Sumi come along. Now instead of the quiet sounds of the wind in the fields, they heard the busy sound of bulldozers and trucks and men hard at work.

Whenever Sumi went to watch the laying of the tracks, she always stopped at Mr. Oda's on the way home to tell him how the work was coming along.

As she entered his yard, Saburo often came to greet her, and she would call out, "Spread your tail, Saburo, spread your tail!" And sometimes he would surprise her by making an enormous multi-colored fan of himself.

To Miki, however, she had nothing to say, for she certainly wasn't going to ask for any more of her milk. "If you could only do something exciting," she would say, but Miki went right on nibbling at the ground and paid no attention to her at all.

"The express will be coming soon," Sumi would say to Mr. Oda, and she usually added, "but it won't stop here."

Mr. Oda always listened very carefully to whatever news Sumi had for him. He stroked his long white beard and nodded solemnly. "It does seem rather unfriendly of it not to stop even once," he said.

Sumi nodded. Mr. Oda was right. It was most unfriendly of it to speed by as though Sugi Village didn't even exist, especially when it was going to pass so close it would rattle the windows of their school house. More and more Sumi began to think of the train as the Unfriendly Express.

Before long, the tracks were laid like a shiny silver band along the rim of the village. And finally, one cold morning of the new year, when the snow on the ground had turned to ice, the first express came through on a trial run. The whole school went out into the yard to watch it go by. It was a beautiful, gleaming blue-and-cream-colored train, and it glided on the rails like a sled on ice, making only a *Whinnnnnng* sound as it raced by.

The children all shouted and waved, but the train sped by without even slowing down. It was hard to tell if anyone was even on board, for no friendly hand waved back to them.

"Imagine," Mr. Mayor said looking pleased, "a little bit of the world beyond will visit us every day."

Each day now they listened for the sound of the express: first the northbound *Whinnnnnng* and then the southbound *Whinnnnnng*.

At first the children craned their necks to look out the window whenever the express went by. But after a few weeks, they forgot to wait or listen anymore, for the Tokyo Express became just another of the daily sounds of the village.

When Sumi woke up one cold morning, the deep furry silence in the air told her that it was snowing. All night the snow had fallen, and the wind had blown it in great drifts that leaned up against houses and trees and made weird white shapes in the fields.

Sumi and Taro put on their warmest winter clothing and their boots and mittens and tramped slowly through the thick snow to school.

It was almost time for Mr. Mayor to ask if anyone had any interesting news to tell when Sumi noticed the strange sound. It was not the usual *Whinnnnnng* of the northbound express, but more of a soft *Whuuuuuuf* sound. And then there was a long silence. Sumi stretched her neck and looked out the window. There, just one hundred yards from their school, stood the Tokyo Express. It was not moving one single inch. It just stood still. The express had actually stopped at Sugi Village.

Sumi didn't even raise her hand or stand up beside her desk. She simply shouted in her loudest voice, "Mr. Mayor, Mr. Mayor, the express has stopped!"

Everyone, including Mr. Mayor, ran to the window. Sure enough, there was the blue-and-cream-colored express standing very still. And in front of it, standing on the tracks, seemed to be an animal. Was it a cow? Sumi thought she saw a spot of red on its head. Could it be her hat? Could it possibly be Miki way out there?

"Come on, children," Mr. Mayor called. "Let's go!"

No one had to be told what to do. Everyone tumbled out into the hall to put on coats and boots and hats. At the last moment, Mr. Mayor remembered to get his ceremonial top hat which he kept in the cupboard beside the blackboard. He wore it only on special occasions when he wanted to look official and mayor-like. Surely this was such an occasion, he thought. After all, it wasn't every day that the express from Tokyo stopped in Sugi Village. And indeed, it might never stop here again, ever.

Sumi thought it was too bad Mr. Mayor wasn't wearing his striped pants and his frock coat too. But she was glad he put on his silky black top hat. He looked very elegant, she thought, even though he had big rubber boots on his feet.

They all ran, pell-mell, stumbling through the snow-covered schoolyard and down the snowy paths that cut through the rice fields. The boys reached the train first, but Sumi was the first of the girls, and Mr. Mayor was right behind her.

"*Yah!* Tokyo Express!" the boys shouted.

"You finally stopped!" Sumi shouted. "You finally stopped!"

Then she ran to the front of the train and saw her old red hat. There it was, sitting on Miki's head as she calmly searched for grass along the railroad tracks.

"Miki!" Sumi shouted. "Did you stop the Tokyo Express?"

As usual, Miki paid no attention to her and went right on nibbling at the snow.

Now a door slid open and one of the train's conductors waved to the children.

Mr. Mayor bowed and removed his top hat. "Welcome to Sugi Village," he called out.

The conductor bowed back and smiled. "If it weren't for her red hat, we probably never would have seen that silly goat," he said good-naturedly. "Now that we've stopped for her, we'll wait here for thirty minutes while they clear the tracks up ahead."

The children edged up to the train and touched its icy cold metal sides. They jumped up and down and tried to look inside the windows.

"Some of the children have never been on a train," Mr. Mayor explained.

"I see," the conductor said.

"Of course, none of them have ever been on a Tokyo Express," Mr. Mayor went on, pressing closer to the door.

The conductor sucked in his breath and thought for a moment. He seemed to know exactly what was going on inside Mr. Mayor's head.

"It would be highly irregular," he said slowly, "and I suppose I could be fired for doing it, but well . . . we have only a few passengers on board, and we may never stop here again."

He beckoned to the children. "Come on," he called. "There's time for a quick look if you hurry."

By now all the children of the school had seen the express and they came running out to see it. Taro and his classmates were soon climbing on board too.

Sumi had never seen anything so new and shiny and beautiful. The windows were wide, with soft gray curtains that could be drawn to keep out the sun. The chairs were comfortable and roomy and leaned back so you could sleep in them. There were adjustable foot rests for your feet and little tables that folded up into the arm rests.

The conductor led them through the first class cars and then into the buffet car. Girls in blue uniforms and white aprons were preparing a cart of food to take through the train. Sumi smelled hot coffee and steaming curry that made her mouth water, and she saw real roses in small glass vases.

It was like another world, this warm bit of comfort and luxury that stood in the midst of the frozen fields. Sumi took a deep breath in order to keep part of it inside of her, for a while at least.

The conductor looked at the big gold watch which he took from his pocket. "All right, children," he said. "Time for everyone to get off. We'll be leaving soon and we can't take you with us. Did someone move that goat from the tracks?"

The children hurried off the train and Sumi ran to get Miki. She straightened her red hat, got a firm grip on her tether, and pulled her quickly from the tracks.

"Come on, Miki," she said. "You really did something exciting today, you did!"

Sumi could hear a voice on the train's loudspeaker announcing that the express would be under way in three minutes. Mr. Mayor took out his watch and waited with it in his hand. In exactly three minutes the door slid to, there was a loud blast of the train's horn, and the express began to glide northward.

"Good-bye, Sugi Village!" the conductor called.

"Good-bye, Tokyo Express!" the children shouted.

"Thank you," Mr. Mayor said, waving his top hat.

And then it was gone, and there were only the shiny tracks left to remind them that the express would come through again the next morning.

"It will never stop again," Sumi said sadly.

"But it stopped once," Mr. Mayor said, "and that is something."

Sumi nodded. It was true. And Miki was the one who had done it.

"*Banzai* for Miki!" Taro shouted.

And everyone gathered around and wanted to touch her shaggy sides—even Ayako. She told Sumi that as soon as she got home, she was going to tell her father about Miki so he could tell everyone in the village what she had done.

Somehow her classmates seemed to think that Sumi was remarkable too, because she was a friend of Miki, the goat. They looked at her as though she were very special, and she was excused from class so she could take Miki back to Mr. Oda. It was a great honor, Sumi thought.

She led Miki carefully down the snowy paths safely to Mr. Oda's yard, and then she tied her with two double knots to the plum tree. Now that she was such a famous goat, she must not be allowed to run away again.

Sumi hurried inside. She could hardly wait to tell the old man what had happened.

"Miki stopped the Tokyo Express!" she shouted in her loudest voice.

Mr. Oda, who was dozing peacefully beside his warm brazier, awoke with a start. "What? What?" he asked in a small thin voice, blinking away the sleep in his eyes.

Still shouting because she couldn't stop, Sumi told him how Miki had stopped the Tokyo Express and how they had all been invited on board to see what it was like inside.

"Ah, ah," the old man said, nodding happily. "And what was it like, this Tokyo Express?"

"It was shiny and new . . . and beautiful and clean," Sumi said, closing her eyes so she could remember. "It was as warm as springtime and it smelled as good as New Year's."

Sumi could find no more words, but the old man understood. "I see," he said. "I see." And his face crumpled into hundreds of wrinkles as he laughed with pleasure.

He called his housekeeper and asked for his cloak and his hat. "We must go tell Miki what a fine thing she did," he said.

"It is cold out," the housekeeper warned, "and the snow is deep."

But the old man did not care. "What is a little snow on such a day?" he asked, and he put on his fur hat and his black cloak and hobbled out into the yard holding Sumi's hand.

Miki stood calmly beside her plum tree, looking as though she had been standing there all day.

"Well, well, Miki," the old man said, reaching out to touch her head. "You are quite a special goat now. I imagine long after I am gone, Sugi Village will remember you for stopping the Tokyo Express."

Miki went right on nibbling, but Sumi no longer wished that Miki was anything other than her own shaggy self. Nor did she wish that she would do something more exciting than give milk. After all, she had done something today that no one else in all of Sugi Village could do—not even Mr. Mayor. And that was more than you could say about any goat.

Sumi edged up close to Miki's ear. "You are a wonderful goat, Miki," she whispered. "You really are."

Miki stopped nibbling and looked up at Sumi's face. Sumi grinned and patted her gently on the head. She knew at last that Miki had listened, and she was sure that this time she had understood.

Zamani Goes to Market

MURIEL L. FEELINGS

It was cool in the early morning. The sun spread a soft light over the family compound of five huts.

Zamani was wide awake. He had slept little that night; he was too excited. Today for the first time he would go to market with Father and his older brothers!

He was already dressed when he heard Mother call: "Wake up, my child. We must get busy."

Mother was cooking over the big pots on the fire. Zamani went to her side and knelt politely. "Have your porridge, then we can prepare," she said, and filled his wooden bowl with ugali.

Zuri, his older sister, came up to him. "Good morning, Zamani." She smiled. "You will not stay with us today."

"No, I am going to market," Zamani said proudly.

In no time his bowl was empty. Looking around, he saw that everyone was busy. Zuri was washing bowls and pots. He saw Father in the distance leading a big steer in from the field. Jenga and Kamili, his brothers, were tying bundles of corn and sacks of cassava.

Mother was gathering clay pots in front of her hut. The large brown pots sparkled in the morning sunlight. Zamani helped her to line them up by size as he had done before. He held each pot steady as she tied them together, neck-to-neck, with heavy string made of sisal plant. Then, carefully, they put them into straw baskets.

"There!" said Mother, satisfied. "We are finished. Thank you for your hands, Zamani."

"Where may I put these, Mother?" he asked.

Mother pointed to the group of trees at the edge of the compound. "If you can do it, they should be carried out there."

To show everyone how strong he could be, Zamani took hold of each basket and slowly dragged them across the compound until he reached the big trees.

Father was nearby loading bundles on the back of the long-horn steer.

Zamani walked over and knelt politely. "Good morning, Father," he greeted shyly.

"Greetings," Father replied. "Are you now too tired to do more?"

"Oh no, Father," Zamani answered, quickly rising to his feet.

"Well, you will have a big job today. Go to the field and bring the brown calf. You will lead it to market."

The brown calf! Zamani dashed off toward the field, grinning with pride. "So," he thought to himself, "I will take goods to market just like Kamili and Jenga!"

As he reached the fenced pen where the four calves grazed, Zamani's steps slowed. He began to feel a big sadness, too. He had seen other calves go to market when he stayed behind. But the brown calf was special to him. He remembered the early, early morning Father had called him from sleep to see this calf when it was just born.

The brown calf turned and wagged its tail as Zamani approached. He led it out of the pen and through the field, guiding it gently with a crooked stick. As he looked back at the others, he told himself that they would take the calf's place. And more would be born.

Father stood waiting, puffing on his old wooden pipe. Jenga and Kamili lifted the baskets of pots onto their shoulders. Everyone was ready to go.

They called good-bye to Mother and Zuri and started down the path through the village to the main road. Father went first, leading the big steer, with Zamani keeping the calf close behind. Then followed Jenga and Kamili.

Zamani turned his head as he heard a familiar voice. Waving to him from the edge of the last village compound was Husein. Zamani waved back. Husein was younger and could not yet go the two miles to market with his father.

Along the road were others of their village, also off to buy and sell. Zamani saw men leading cattle, women with babies strapped to their backs and carrying large wide baskets on their heads. One boy of Jenga's age was busy juggling two huge baskets of squawking chickens.

Suddenly Zamani felt a *bump*. It was the calf! Zamani gave it a pat on the shoulder and kept a closer watch.

"One half-mile more," Kamili called from behind.

Nearly there! Holding the calf tight, Zamani darted out into the middle of the road to see what was ahead. He strained his eyes hard, past the crowd, and looked and looked. In the distance, he could see tiny low buildings and other taller ones. *"Kuja, Kuja!"* He urged the calf into a faster pace.

Soon they were walking through the wide street of the town. When they reached the entrance to the market grounds, the long parade of people went in all directions.

The market was just coming alive. Many vendors were still filling their stalls. Others called: "Good mats!" "Gourds here!" "Good pots!" "Buy here!" Smells of mangoes, pineapples, oranges, and roasting meats filled the air.

Kamili and Jenga went off to sell their pots to those who did not make them.

Father led the way to the far end of the big market where animals were bought and sold. Zamani followed him, guiding the calf through the crowd.

Father stopped at the gate of a tall bamboo fence. Behind it, the sounds of cattle, goats, and chickens could be heard. The brown calf became restless hearing the familiar animal noises. Zamani had to hold it firmly.

A tall fat man came through the gate. He walked around the steer and calf, frowning and touching them here and there, mumbling to himself.

"These are as good as always," Father said. He offered to sell the corn and cassava also.

The fat man continued to look and touch as if he hadn't heard. He and Father began to argue over the price.

Finally, Zamani saw the fat man throw up his hands as if to say, "You win!" Zamani felt proud that his father had won.

The man reached into a large wooden box and handed Father some paper money. Zamani watched as he led the steer and calf away. He hoped the calf would be well cared for and grow up as beautifully as the steer.

As he and Father walked to the sheltered part of the market, they were joined by Kamili and Jenga.

"Here is the money earned from the pots, Father," said Jenga. The two boys handed him several coins. Father returned three to each, and they ran down the aisle to buy.

"You too have done your share of the day's work," Father said to Zamani. He handed him two coins. "What would you like to buy?"

Zamani looked at the stalls around him. So many things for sale! Straw mats of all sizes and colors. Shoes. Rows of brightly colored ornaments and bead-covered gourds. Stacks of cloth and new kanzus—long, white robes like those his brothers wore. "I don't know yet, Father," he said.

"Well," Father replied, "you will learn to buy wisely today. What do you want most?"

Zamani thought and thought. He stopped before a row of leather sandals of red and brown. He went to another stall where clean, white kanzus were hanging. One, his size, was decorated with orange braid around the collar. Yes, that was just the thing to buy! It would be his first kanzu.

He turned to tell Father, but then, across the aisle, he saw a beautiful necklace. It was made of three rows of beads—orange, yellow, and white—strung on fine wire into a circular shape. Zamani thought of his mother, who always remembered to bring him sugar cane from the market. He looked back at the kanzu with the orange braid, then at the necklace. Finally he decided.

"I will buy beads for Mother," he said to Father.

"Let us see what the cost is," Father replied. "How much is this one?" he asked the tiny woman behind the counter.

"One shilling, sir."

Zamani looked at the coins in his hand. He had exactly the amount of the necklace. Two fifty-cent coins. "I will buy this necklace," he said to the lady.

She wrapped the necklace in a piece of cloth and tied it neatly with banana-fiber string.

Zamani handed her the coins, then tucked the bundle into the waist of his toga. Suddenly he felt very pleased. He had made his first purchase. He would give his first gift from the market.

Jenga and Kamili joined them, each with a package under his arm.

"You three may head back home," Father said. "I must buy grain for the month and will meet you later on the road."

Zamani followed his brothers down the aisle. The market was now very crowded, and they had to weave in and out among the groups of people. Sometimes Zamani bumped against baskets over the arms of busy shoppers. He began to feel very small in that large, noisy market. But, even so, it was fun!

Then they were out of the market and town, and on the road leading home.

It was nearly midday. The soft breezes from the great lake cooled their cheeks as they walked. When the market had grown small in the distance, Zamani remembered the package he had tucked away.

"Kamili, Jenga! See what I bought today!" he cried,

boasting. Kneeling down on the ground, he pulled out the flat package from the waist of his toga and untied the string. He carefully unfolded the piece of cloth and held up the sparkling necklace.

"Oh ho! So you wear a necklace now!" joked Kamili, clapping his hands. Jenga laughed too.

"No, no! It is a gift for Mother. Will she like it?" Zamani asked eagerly.

"Oh yes, she will be quite pleased. She has none like it," assured Jenga. "And what else did you buy, little one?"

"That is all," Zamani answered. "What did you bring?"

The boys unfolded their bundles. Kamili had a new straw mat of green and brown. Jenga showed a long white kanzu with orange braid around the neck.

"Just like the one I saw!" Zamani thought, as he ran his hand over the cloth.

Father caught up with them as they were retying their bundles. He was carrying a heavy sack and a smaller bundle.

"You certainly did not get far," he said jokingly. "I thought you would be halfway home!"

As they walked, many people passed them on the left in automobiles, on bicycles, and on foot. Others were also headed back home in their direction. Father greeted villagers and they talked as they went along the sunny road.

At last they were home. Mother and Zuri were preparing the afternoon meal, and the pots were steaming on the fire.

Everyone washed quickly, and Mother served each a large bowl of ugali and stew. She carried one to Father who sometimes ate inside in the heat of the afternoon. Then she returned to the fireside and sat to eat with her four children, and to talk of the news of the market place.

Zamani could not eat his food fast enough. He was anxious to tell his surprise.

"Zamani!" laughed Mother. "Why do you rush so?"

"I must show you something!"

"Well, I hope this *something* will not fly away before you have eaten," she joked, and everyone laughed.

"No, Mother," Zamani answered. He glanced at his two brothers.

Kamili and Jenga smiled at him, put down their empty bowls, and went off to tend the cattle in the field.

Zamani reached into his waistband, pulled out the little flat bundle, and held it out for Mother. "Here is something for you," he said.

"For me?" Mother asked, surprised. She untied the string and unfolded the wrapping. "Oh!" she exclaimed aloud. She held up the bright necklace. "Zuri! Zuri!" See what my son has brought me!"

Zuri came and looked at the necklace Mother was

proudly holding. "Oh-eh! It was the most beautiful in the market!" she praised.

"Thank you, Zamani," Mother said, and she cupped his face in her hands.

Zamani smiled, with eyes cast downward.

All the family now prepared to go to work. Father, with his hoe over one shoulder, went off to dig in the cornfield. Mother went to her cassava garden nearby, and Zuri was busily scrubbing pots from the afternoon meal.

Zamani's job was to sweep the compound grounds. He went to his hut for the broom.

Inside the cool dark room, he saw a strange object lying on his sleeping mat. His eyes widened as he knelt down to get a closer look. There, on the mat, was a clean new kanzu with orange braid around the neck! Excited, he stood up and held it against his body. It was his size!

He rushed outside, but there was no one to question. He ran back inside and took off his toga. Carefully, he pulled the gown over his head and pushed his arms into the sleeves. He tied it at the neck and walked over into the light of the doorway. Looking down, it was just the right length. He held his head high as he strutted around the hut in his first kanzu. How fine he would look when he entered school.

At last he took off the robe and folded it neatly. As he

began to sweep the compound, he thought and thought. How did the kanzu get there? Then he remembered the small bundle Father had carried under his arm. Yes! It was Father! But how did he know?

Zamani covered every inch of ground with his broom, anxious for evening to come when he would thank Father for the surprise gift. He thought of Father in the field, puffing on his old wooden pipe. "A new gift for Father!" he exclaimed, as he swept the last spot of ground.

He sat down in front of his hut. How could he buy Father a pipe? He would have to make things to sell at the market. Yes, that was it. He would ask Jenga to teach him how to make the brown pots.

Zamani picked up his crooked stick and ran off toward the fields to join his brothers and share his plan for the next market day.

Acknowledgments

Thanks are due to the following for permission to reprint copyrighted works:

Atheneum Publishers for pages 32-47 from *The Leopard* by Cecil Bødker, translation copyright © 1975 by Gunnar Poulsen; and for pages 3-24 of *Roam the Wild Country*, copyright © 1967 by Ella Thorp Ellis.

Thomas Y. Crowell and Penguin Books Ltd. for pages 13-26 from *Hello, Aurora* by Anne-Cath. Vestly, Copyright © 1966 by Tiden Norsk Forlag, translation Copyright © 1973 by Longman Young Books; and "In the Middle of the Night" from *What the Neighbors Did and Other Stories* by Philippa Pearce (Longman Young Books), Copyright © 1959, 1967, 1969, 1972 by Philippa Pearce.

Grosset & Dunlap, Inc. for adaptation of pages 1-36 of *Shurik* by Kyra Petrovskya Wayne, Copyright © 1970 by Kyra Petrovskya Wayne.

Harper & Row, Publishers, Inc. for pages 130-150 of *Far Out the Long Canal* by Meindert DeJong, text Copyright © 1964 by Meindert DeJong; for an abridgment of pages 5-34 from *Julie of the Wolves* by Jean Craighead George, text Copyright © 1972 by Jean Craighead George; for pages 5-31, abridged, from *February Dragon* by Colin Thiele, Copyright © 1966 by Colin Thiele, first published in Australia by Rigby Ltd.

Houghton Mifflin Company for pages 45-53 from *The Black Pearl* by Scott O'Dell, Copyright © 1967 by Scott O'Dell; and pages 79-97 from *The Bushbabies* by William H. Stevenson, Copyright © 1965 by William H. Stevenson.

William Morrow & Company, Inc. for an abridgment of pages 28-60 from *Pulga* by S. R. Van Iterson, original Dutch edition © Ultgeverij Leopold, translation Copyright © 1971 by William Morrow and Company, Inc.